CW01431908

TALES OF LOVE, MADNESS AND DEATH

Selected stories

Horacio Quiroga

ISBN: 9781078184656

DEDICATION

People who seeks dark side from their minds…

CONTENT

ACKNOWLEDGMENT

Writers who made masterpieces for people like me.

A STATION OF LOVE

SPRING

It was the carnival Tuesday. Nébel had just entered the corso, already at dusk, and while unpacking a package of streamers looked at the carriage in front. Missing from a face he had not seen in the car the previous afternoon, he asked his companions:

-Who? It does not look ugly.

-A demon! It is beautiful. I think niece, or something like that, of the doctor Arrizabalaga. It arrived yesterday, I think ...

Nébel then fixed her eyes carefully on the beautiful creature. She was a very young girl still, perhaps no more than fourteen years old, but already nubile. He had, under very dark hair, a face of supreme whiteness, that matt white and satin that is the exclusive patrimony of very fine complexions. Blue eyes, long, losing to the temples between black lashes. Perhaps a little separated, which gives, under a smooth forehead, air of great nobility or great stubbornness. But her eyes, as they were, filled that face in bloom with the light of her beauty. And when Nébel felt detained a moment in his, he was dazzled.

-What a beauty! He murmured, standing motionless with one knee on the surrey's cushion. A moment later the streamers flew toward victory. Both

3

carriages were already linked by the hanging paper bridge, and the one who caused it smiled from time to time at the gallant boy.

But that already came to the lack of respect for people, coachmen and even the carriage: the streamers rained incessantly. So much so, that the two people seated behind turned and, well, smiling, carefully examined the wasteful.

-Who are they? Nébel asked in a low voice.

"Dr. Arrizabalaga ... Certainly you do not know him. The other is the mother of your girl ... She's the doctor's sister-in-law.

As if in pursuit of the examination, Arrizabalaga and the lady smiled frankly at the exuberance of youth, Nébel thought it his duty to greet them, to which the *terceto* replied with jovial condescension.

This was the beginning of an idyll that lasted three months, and to which Nébel believed in the duty to greet them, to which the *terceto* responded with jovial condescension. While the *corso* continued, and in Concordia it lasted until incredible hours, Nébel tended his arm incessantly, so well that the fist of his shirt, detached, danced on the hand.

The next day the scene was reproduced; and as this time the Corsican resumed at night with battle of flowers, Nébel exhausted in a quarter of an hour four immense baskets. Arrizabalaga and the lady laughed, turning their heads often, and the young woman did not turn her eyes away from her head often, and the young woman did not move her eyes away from Nébel. He cast a desperate look at his empty baskets. But on the pillow of the surrey there was still one, a poor bouquet of evergreens and jasmines of the country. Nébel jumped with him on the jasmine wheel of the country. Nébel jumped with him on the wheel of the surrey, dislocated almost an ankle, and running to victory, panting, drenched in sweat and with enthusiasm at the sight of the eyes, he extended the bouquet to the young man. She looked dumbly for another, but she did not have it. His companions laughed.

-But crazy! The mother said, pointing to her chest . There you have one!

The carriage started at a trot. Nébel, who had descended afflicted from the stirrup, ran and reached for the bouquet that the young woman tended with her body almost out of the car.

Nébel had arrived three days ago from Buenos Aires, where he finished his baccalaureate. He had stayed there for seven years, so that his knowledge of the current society of Concordia was minimal. He must still stay for fifteen days in his native city, enjoyed in full tranquility of soul, but of body. And behold, from the second day he lost all his serenity. But instead, what a charm!

-What a beauty! -It was repeated thinking about that ray of light, flower and female flesh that had come to him from the carriage. He recognized himself real and deeply dazzled - and in love, of course.

And if she wanted it! ... Would she want it? Nébel, to elucidate him, trusted much more than in the bouquet of his chest, in the dazed precipitation with which the young woman had looked for something to give him. He clearly evoked the brightness of his eyes when he saw him come running, the restless expectation with which he waited for him - and in another order, the morbidity of the young chest, when he handed her the bouquet.

And now, concluded! She was leaving the next day to Montevideo. What did he care about the rest, Concordia, his old friends, his father? At least he would go with her to Buenos Aires.

They actually made the trip together, and during it Nébel came to the highest degree of passion that a romantic eighteen-year-old boy who feels loved can reach. The mother welcomed the almost infantile idyll with affable complacency, and laughed often when she saw them, talking little, smiling incessantly and looking at herself infinitely.

The farewell was short, because Nébel did not want to lose the last vestige of sanity he had left, cutting his career after her.

They would return to Concordia in the winter, perhaps a season. Would he go? "Oh, I do not return!" And while Nébel walked slowly down the dock, turning at every moment, she, chest on the rail and head down, followed him with her eyes, while on the ironing the sailors raised the His smiling faces to that idyll- and to the dress, still short, of the tender bride.

SUMMER
[I]

On the 13th of June Nébel returned to Concordia, and although she knew from the first moment that Lydia was there, she spent a week without worrying a little or a lot about her. Four months are ample time for a flash of passion, and hardly in the sleeping water of his soul the last glow reached to curl his self-love. I felt, yes, curious to see her. Until a small incident, puncturing his vanity, dragged him back. On the first Sunday, Nébel, like every good guy in village, waited at the corner for the departure of mass. At last, the last perhaps, erect and looking forward, Lidia and her mother moved through the line of boys.

Nébel, upon seeing her again, felt his eyes expand to suck the abruptly adored figure in all its fullness. He waited with almost painful anxiety the moment when her eyes, in a sudden flash of happy surprise, would recognize him among the group.

But it happened, with his cold gaze fixed ahead.

"It seems he does not remember you anymore, " said a friend, who had followed the incident at his side.

-Not much! He smiled . And it's a pity, because I really liked the girl.

But when he was alone he cried to himself his misfortune. And now that he had seen her again! How, how he had always wanted her, he who thought he did not remember anymore! And finished! Pum, pum, pum! He repeated without realizing . Pum! Everything is over!

Suddenly: What if they had not seen me? ... Sure! but of course! His face brightened again, and he welcomed this vague probability with deep conviction.

At three o'clock he beat at the house of Dr. Arrizabalaga. His idea was elementary:

I would consult with any miserable pretext to the lawyer; and perhaps I saw it.

It was there. A sudden race through the courtyard responded to the bell, and Lidia, to stop the impulse, had to cling violently to the stained glass door. He saw Nébel, he exclaimed, and hiding with his arms the lightness of his clothes, fled even faster.

A moment later the mother opened the office, and welcomed her former acquaintance with more complacency with greater complacency than four months ago. Nébel did not have joy in himself; and since the lady did not seem to be bothered by Nébel's legal concerns, he also preferred that presence a million times to that of the lawyer.

Yet he was on the embers of too hot a happiness. And since he was eighteen years old, he wanted to leave at once so that he could enjoy his immense happiness alone and without shortness.

- Soon, now! Said the lady . I hope we'll have the pleasure of seeing it again ... Is not it? ... is not true?

- Oh, yes, ma'am!

- At home we would all have a lot of pleasure ... I guess everyone! Do you want us to consult? -He smiled with motherly mockery.

-Oh, with all my soul! Replied Nébel.

-Lidia! Come here a minute! There is a person here that you know.

Lidia arrived when he was already on his feet. He advanced to meet Nébel, his eyes sparkling with happiness, and handed her a large bouquet of violets, with adorable awkwardness.

"If you do not mind, " the mother continued , "you could come every Monday ... What do you think?"

- That is very little, lady! The boy replied . Fridays also, can I?

The lady laughed.

-What a hurry! I do not know ... Let's see what Lidia says. What do you say, Lidia?

The creature, who did not turn away his laughing eyes from Nébel, said yes! in the face, since he owed his answer.

-Very well: then until Monday, Nébel.

Nébel objected:

- Would not you allow me to come tonight? Today is an extraordinary day ...

-Good! Tonight too! Accompany him, Lidia.

But Nébel, in a mad need for movement, said goodbye right there and fled with her bouquet whose rope she had almost undone, and with the soul projected to the last heaven of happiness.

[II]

For two months, in all the moments they were seen, in all the hours that separated them, Nébel and Lidia adored each other. For him, romantic to feel the state of painful melancholy that provokes a simple dribble that *agrisa* the patio, the creature that, with its angelic face, its blue eyes and its early plenitude, had to embody the possible sum of ideal. For her, Nébel was manly, handsome and intelligent. There was no cloud in their mutual love other than Nebel's minority. The boy, leaving aside studies, careers and other superfluities, wanted to get married. As proven, there were only two things: that it was absolutely impossible for him to live without Lydia, and that he would take everything he opposed to it before him. I sensed - or rather said, felt - that I was going to skate roughly.

His father, in fact, whom he had profoundly disliked the year that Nébel lost after a carnival affair, had to point out the i's with terrible vigor. At the end of August, one day he spoke definitively to his son:

-I have been told that you are following your visits to Arrizabalaga. It is true? Because you do not deign to tell me a word.

Nébel saw the whole storm in that form of dignity, and his voice trembled a little when he answered:

-If I did not say anything to you, dad, it's because I know you do not like me to talk about it. -Bah! As you like it, you can, in effect, save your work ... But

I would like to know in what state you are. Are you going to that house as a boyfriend?

-Yes.

- And they receive you formally?

-I think so...

The father stared at him and drummed on the table.

-It's good! Very good! ... Listen to me, because I have a duty to show you the way. Do you know what you're doing well? Have you thought about what can happen?

- Pass? ... What?

-That you marry that girl. But look: you're old enough to reflect, at least.

Do you know who it is? Where does it come from? Do you know anyone who knows what life they have in Montevideo?

-Father!

-Yes, what are you doing there! Bah! Do not put that face ... I do not mean your ... girlfriend.

That is a creature, and as such does not know what it does. But do you know what they live?

-Do not! I do not care, because even if you're my father ...

-Bah, bah, bah! Leave that for later. I do not speak to you as a father but as any honest man could speak to you. And since it makes you so angry about what I'm asking you, find out whoever wants to tell you, what kind of relationships your girlfriend's mother has with her brother-in-law, ask!

-Yes! I know it has been ...

-Ah, do you know what has been Arrizabalaga's mistress? And what about him or someone else holding the house in Montevideo? And you stay so cool!

-...!

-Yes, I know! Your girlfriend has nothing to do with this, I know! There is no more beautiful impulse than yours ... But be careful, because you can be late ... No, no, calm down! I have no idea of offending your girlfriend, I think, as I told you, that she is not there. Contaminated, even by the rot that surrounds it. But if the mother wants to sell it to you in marriage, or rather to the fortune

that you are going to inherit when I die, tell her that old Nébel is not disposed to those traffics and that the devil will take him before to consent to that marriage. Nothing the devil to consent to that. I just wanted to tell you.

The boy loved his father very much, in spite of his father, despite his character; he went out full of rage for not being able to vent his anger, all the more violent because he himself knew he was unjust. It had been a long time since I did not ignore it. Lidia's mother had been loved by Arrizabalaga during her husband's life, and even four or five years later. They were still seen from

time to time, but the old libertine, now wrapped in his sickly bachelor arthritis, was far from being what he wanted to be about his sister-in-law; and if he kept the train of mother and daughter, he did it for a kind of gratitude of ex-lover, and on a kind of compassion for ex-lover, and above all to authorize the current gossip that inflated his vanity.

Nébel evoked the mother; and with a shudder of a crazy boy for married women, he remembered a certain night when, leafing through together and reclining an "Illustration," he had thought that on his suddenly tense nerves there was a deep breath of desire that came from the full body that brushed against him. When lifting his eyes, Nébel had seen her look, dizzy, perch heavily on his.

He was wrong? It was terribly hysterical, but with rare explosive crises; the disordered nerves rattled inward and hence the sickly tenacity in a nonsense and the sudden abandonment of a conviction; and in the *pródromos* of the crises, the growing, convulsive obstinacy, edifying itself with great blocks of absurdities. Abused morphine by harrowing need and elegance. He was thirty-seven years old; It was tall, with very thick and lighted lips that moistened incessantly.

Without being big, his eyes seemed to him by the cut and by having very long eyelashes; but they were admirable of shadow and fire. It was painted. He dressed, like the daughter, with perfect good taste, and this was undoubtedly his greatest seduction. He must have had, as a woman, profound charm; now hysteria had worked her body a lot - being, of course, sick to her belly. When
the whiplash of morphine passed, his eyes blurred, and from the corners of his lips, from the globose eyelid, hung a thin net of wrinkles.
But in spite of that, the same hysteria that undid his nerves was the slightly magical food that sustained his tonicity.

I dearly loved Lydia; and with the morale of the hysterical bourgeoisie, she would have degraded her daughter to make her happy- that is, to provide her with what would have made her own happiness.
Thus, the restlessness of Nébel's father in this regard touched his son in the depths of his strings of his lover's strings. How had Lydia escaped? Because the limpidity of her complexion, the frankness of her girl's passion that arose with adorable freedom from her bright eyes, was, no longer a test of purity, but a step of noble joy for which Nébel ascended triumphantly to tear away the rotten plant, the flower that he asked for.

This conviction was so intense that Nébel had never kissed her. One afternoon, after lunch, when I was going through Arrizabalaga, I had felt a crazy desire to see her. Her happiness was complete, for she found her alone, in baton, and the curls on her cheeks. As Nébel held her against the wall, she, laughing and cut, leaned against the wall. And the boy, to his forehead, touching her almost, felt in his inert hands the high happiness of an immaculate love, which would have been so easy to stain him.
But then, once his wife! Nébel precipitated as much as possible his marriage. Her qualification of age, obtained in those days, allowed her for her legitimate mother to face the expenses. The consent of the father remained, and the mother urged this detail.

The situation of her, overrun in Concordia, required a social sanction that should begin, of course, for the future father-in-law of her daughter. And above all, she was sustained by the desire to humiliate, to force bourgeois morals to bend her knees before the same inconvenience that she despised.

Several times he had touched the point with his future son-in-law, with allusions to "my father-in-law" ... "my new family" ..., "my daughter's sister-in-law". Nébel was silent, and the mother's eyes shone then with more *sombre* fire.

Until one day the flame rose. Nébel had set October 18 for her marriage. It was still more than a month away, but the mother clearly understood the boy who wanted his father's presence that night.

"It will be difficult, " Nébel said after a mortifying silence . It costs a lot to go out at night ... It never comes out.

-Ah! Exclaimed only the mother, quickly biting her lip. Another pause followed, but this one of omen.

-Because you do not make a clandestine marriage, right? -Oh! Nébel smiled

hard . My father does not believe it either. -And so?

New silence, increasingly stormy.

"Is it because of me that your father does not want to attend?

-No, no, ma'am! "Nébel exclaimed at last, impatiently. " It's in his way of being ... I'll talk to him again, if he wants.

-I want? The mother smiled, dilating her nostrils . Do what you want ... Do you want to leave, Nébel, now? I'm not well.

Nébel came out, deeply displeased. What was he going to say to his father? He always maintained his strong opposition to such a marriage, and the son had already taken steps to do without it.

-You can do that, and whatever you want. But my consent for that entertaining to be your mother-in-law, never!

After three days Nébel decided to conclude a decision to clarify at once this time with this state of affairs, and took advantage of it for a moment when Lidia was not.

"I spoke with my father," Nébel began , "and he told me that it would be completely impossible for him to attend.

The mother became a little pale, while her eyes, in a sudden flash, stretched towards the temples.

-Ah! And because?

"I do not know, " Nébel said in a low voice.

- That is ... that your father is afraid of getting stained if he puts his feet here.

-I don't know! He repeated, stubborn in turn.

-It is a gratuitous offense that makes us that man! What have you figured? She added, her voice already altered and her lips trembling . Who is he to give that tone?

Nébel then felt the shock of reaction in the deep strain of his family.

-What is it, I do not know! He said, his voice hasty in turn . But not only does he refuse to attend, he does not give his consent either.

-What? What is denied? And because? Who is he? The most authorized for this!

Nébel got up:

-You are not...

But she had risen too.

-If he! You are a creature! Ask him where he got his fortune, stolen from his customers! And with those airs! His irreproachable family, without blemish, fills his mouth with that! Your family! ...

Tell him to tell you how many walls he had to jump to go to sleep with your woman before getting married! Yes, and he comes with his family!

... Very well, leave; I'm up to here with hypocrisy! Have a good time!

[III]

Nébel lived four days in the deepest despair. What could I expect after what happened? At the fifth, and at nightfall, he received a note:

«Octavio: Lidia is quite ill, and only her presence could calm her down. María S. de Arrizabalaga »

It was a trick, it offered no doubt. But if your Lidia really ...

It was that night, and the mother received him with a discretion that astonished Nébel: without excessive affability, nor with the air of a sinner who apologizes.

-If you want to see her ...

Nébel entered with the mother, and saw her adored love in bed, her face with that freshness without powders that only give the fourteen years, and the legs collected.

He sat down beside her, and in vain the mother waited for something to be said: they only looked at each other and smiled.

Suddenly Nébel felt that they were alone, and the image of the mother came out clearly: "He goes so that in the transport of my reconquered love he loses his head, and marriage is thus forced." But in that quarter of an hour of final enjoyment that was offered to him at the expense of a marriage promissory note, the eighteen-year-old boy felt - like again against the wall – pleasure without the slightest stain, of a pure love in all his Aura of poetic idyll.

Only Nébel could say how great was his happiness recovered after the shipwreck. He also forgot what was in the mother explosion of slander, angry desire to insult those who do not deserve it. But he had the coldest decision to remove the mother from his life, once they were married. The memory of his tender girlfriend, pure and laughing in the bed that had been tipped aside for him, lit the promise of a full voluptuousness, which had not prematurely stolen the smallest diamond.

The next night, on arriving at Arrizabalaga, Nébel found the dark hallway. After a long time the servant opened the window.

-Have they come out? He asked, surprised.

-No, they are going to Montevideo ... They have gone to the Salto to sleep

on board. -Ah! Murmured Nébel terrified. I had hope yet. -The doctor? I can

talk with him?

-No this; He has gone to the club after eating.

Once alone in the dark street, Nébel raised and dropped his arms with deadly discouragement: It's all over! His happiness, his happiness reconquered a day before, lost again and forever! I sensed that this time there was no possible redemption. The nerves of the mother had jumped crazy, like keys, and he could not do more.

He walked to the corner, and from there, motionless under the lantern, stared stupidly at the pink house. He went around the block, and stopped again under the lantern. Never, never again!

Until eleven thirty he did the same. At last he went home and loaded the revolver. But a memory stopped him: months ago he had promised a German cartoonist that before committing suicide one day - Nébel was a teenager - he would go to see him. Unite him with the old soldier of Guillermo a living friendship, based on long philosophical talks.

The next morning, very early, Nébel called the poor room of that one. The expression on his face was too explicit.

-Is now? The paternal friend asked him, shaking his hand tightly.

-Pst! Anyway! ... "the boy replied, looking away.

The draftsman, with great calm, told him then his own drama of love. "Go home, " he concluded , "and if you have not changed your mind by eleven o'clock, come back." to have lunch with me, if we have what. Then he will do what he wants. He swears?

" I swear, " Nébel replied, returning her narrow squeeze with a great desire to cry. A Lidia card was waiting for him in his house: «*Idolatrado Octavio*:

My despair cannot be greater. But Mama has seen that if I married you, great sorrows were reserved for me, I understood as she did that the best thing was to separate us and she swears never to forget it you Lidia"

-Oh, it had to be like that! Cried the boy, seeing at the same time with horror his face, which was in the mirror. It was the mother who had inspired the letter, her and her damn madness! Lidia could not help writing, and the poor girl, upset, cried all her love in the newsroom . Oh! If I could see her one day, tell her how I loved her, how much I love her now, adored by my soul! ...

Trembling, he went to the night table and picked up the revolver, but he remembered his new promise, and for a very long time he stood there, stubbornly cleaning the drum with his fingernail.

AUTUMN

One afternoon, in Buenos Aires, Nébel ended up getting on the tram when the car stopped a moment longer than the convenience, and Nébel, who was reading, finally turned his head.

A woman with a slow and difficult step moved between the seats. After a quick glance at the uncomfortable person, Nébel resumed reading. The lady sat next to him, and as she did so, she looked at her neighbor closely. Nébel, although from time to time she felt the foreign gaze resting on him, continued reading it; but finally he got tired and raised his strange face.

"I thought it was you, " the lady exclaimed , "although I still doubted ... You do not remember me, do you?

"Yes , " said Nébel, opening his eyes. "Madame de Arrizabalaga ...
She saw the surprise of Nébel, and smiled with an air of an old courtesan who is still trying to look good to a boy.

Of her - when Nébel met her eleven years ago - there were only the eyes, although more sunken, and already extinguished. The yellow skin, with shades of green in the shadows, cracked in dusty furrows. The cheekbones jumped now, and the lips, always thick, pretended to hide a fully decayed denture.

Under the emaciated body morphine could be seen running through exhausted nerves and watery arteries, until the elegant woman who one day leafed through the "Illustration" at her side became that skeleton.

13

-I am very old ... and sick, I have already had attacks on the kidneys ... And you -he added, looking at him tenderly- , always the same! Truth is that she is not thirty years old yet ... Lidia is also the same.

Nébel looked up:
-Single?
-Yes ... How glad you will be when I tell you! Why does not she give that pleasure to the poor? Do not you want to go see us?
"With pleasure ... " Nébel murmured.
-Yes, go soon; you know what we have been for you ... Anyway, Boedo, 1483; department 14 ... Our position is so petty ...
-Oh! He protested, getting up to leave. He promised to go very soon.
Twelve days later Nébel had to return to the mill, and before that he wanted to fulfill his promise. It was there - a miserable suburb department . Madame de Arrizabalaga received him, while Lidia arranged herself a little.
- So eleven years! The mother observed again . As time goes!

And you who could have an infinity of children with Lydia!
" Surely, " Nébel smiled, looking around.
-Oh! We are not very well! And above all, how his house should be set up ... I always hear about his cane fields ... Is that his only establishment?
-Yes ... In Entre Ríos too ...
-So happy! If I could one ... Always wanting to spend a few months in the field, and always with desire!
He paused, glancing at Nébel. This one, with a tight heart, clearly relived the impressions buried eleven years in his soul.
-And all this for lack of relationships ... It's so hard to have a friend in those conditions! Nébel's heart was contracting more and more, and Lydia entered.

She was also very changed, because the charm of a candor and a freshness of fourteen years is not found again in the woman of twenty-six. But beautiful always. His masculine sense of smell felt in his morbid neck, in the calm tranquility of his gaze, and in everything indefinable that denounces to man the love already enjoyed, that he must keep veiled forever the memory of the
Lydia he knew.

They talked about very trivial things, with perfect discretion of mature people. When she left again for a moment, the mother resumed:
-Yes, he's a bit weak ... And when I think that in the field he would be right back ... See, Octavio: may I be frank with you? You know I've loved him like a son ... Could not we spend a season in his establishment? How much good he would do to Lydia!

"I 'm married, " said Nébel.

The lady had a gesture of lively annoyance, and for a moment her disappointment was sincere; but then he crossed his comic hands:
- Married, you! Oh, what a disgrace, what a disgrace! Forgive me, you know! ... I do not know what I say ... And your lady lives with you in the mill?
-Yes, generally ... Now it's in Europe.
-What a disgrace! That is ... Octavio! He added, opening his arms with tears in the eyes -: I can tell you, you have been almost my son ... We are little less than in misery!

Why do not you want me to go with Lydia? I'm going to have a mother's confession with you, "she concluded with a doughy smile and lowering her voice. " You know Lidia's heart well, do not you? He waited for an answer, but Nébel remained silent.

-Yes, you know her! And do you think Lidia is a woman capable of forgetting when she wanted to?

Now he had reinforced his suggestion with a slow, slight wink. Nébel then valued suddenly the abyss in which he could have fallen before. She was always the same mother, but already debased by her own old soul, morphine and poverty. And Lidia ... Seeing her again, she had felt a sudden shock of desire for the current woman with a full throat and already shuddering. Before the commercial treaty that was offered, he threw himself into the arms of that rare conquest destined for him.

- Do not you know, Lidia? The mother exclaimed in delight, as her daughter returned . Octavio invites us to spend a season in his establishment. How about?
Lydia had a fugitive contraction of eyebrows and regained her serenity.

-Very good mom ...
-Ah! You do not know what he says? Is married. So young yet! We are almost from his family...
Lidia then turned her eyes to Nébel, and looked at him for a moment with painful gravity.
-Long time? He murmured.
"Four years, " he said softly. In spite of everything, he lacked the courage to look at her.

WINTER
[I]

They did not make the trip together for one last scruple of Nébel in a line where he was well known; but when they left the station they all went up in the house. When Nébel was left alone in the sugar mill, he did not save his domestic servant more than an old Indian woman, because - more than his own frugality - his wife took all the servitude with him. In this way he presented his companions to the faithful native as an old aunt and her daughter, who came to recover lost health.

Nothing more credible, on the other hand, because the lady decayed vertiginously. It had come undone, the foot uncertain and heavy, and in its anguished faces the morphine, which had sacrificed four hours at the behest of Nébel, cried out for a run inside that living corpse. Nébel, who cut his studies at the death of his father, knew enough to foresee a rapid catastrophe; the kidney, intimately attacked, sometimes had dangerous stops that morphine only precipitated.

Already in the car, unable to resist anymore, the lady had looked at Nébel with anguished anguish:

-If you allow me, Octavio ... I cannot take it anymore! Lidia, stand in front.

The daughter quietly hid her mother a little, and Nébel heard the crunch of the clothes violently picked up to prick her thigh. The eyes lit up, and a fullness of life covered that agonized face like a mask.

-Now I'm fine ... What bliss! I feel good.

"I should leave that, " said Nébel harshly, looking at her sideways . When you arrive, it will be worse.

-Oh no! Before dying right here.

Nébel spent the whole day disgusted, and determined to live as long as he could without seeing Lidia and her mother more than two sick poor. But at dusk, and as an example of the beasts that begin at that time to sharpen them begin at that time to sharpen their claws, male zeal began to relax the waist in chills *lasos*.

They ate early, because the mother, broken, wanted to go to bed at once. There was also no means of exclusively taking milk.

-Huy! What disgust! I cannot pass it. And you want me to sacrifice the last years of my life, now that I could die happy?

Lidia did not blink. He had spoken with Nébel few words, and only at the end of the coffee did his gaze get fixed on hers; but Lidia lowered his immediately.

Four hours later, Nébel opened the door of the fourth Lydia without noise.

-Who! The voice was suddenly startled.

"It's me, " murmured Nébel.

A movement of clothes, like that of a person who sits abruptly on the bed, followed his words, and silence reigned again. But when Nebel's hand touched a cool arm in the darkness, the body then trembled in a deep shake...

Then, inert to the side of that woman who had already known love before he arrived, he rose from the innermost recesses of Nébel's soul the holy pride of his adolescence of never having touched, of not having stolen even a kiss, to the creature that looked at him with radiant candor.

He thought about Dostoyevsky's words, which until that moment he had not understood:

"Nothing is more beautiful and stronger in life, than a pure memory." Nébel had kept it, that spotless memory, immaculate purity of his eighteen years, and that now lay there, muddy to the chalice on a maid's bed.

He felt two heavy, silent tears on his neck. She in turn would remember ... And Lydia's tears continued one after the other, watering, like a grave, the abominable end of her only dream of happiness.

[II]

For ten days life went on in common, although Nébel was almost out all day. By tacit agreement, Lidia and he were very rarely alone; and although at night they saw each other again, they were still silent for a long time.

Lydia herself had enough to do taking care of her mother, prostrate at last. As there was no possibility of rebuilding the already rotten, and even to barter the immediate danger it caused.

Nébel thought about suppressing morphine. But she abstained one morning, when, abruptly entering the dining room, she surprised Lidia, who was hurrying down her skirts. He had the syringe in his hand, and he fixed his frightened eyes on Nébel.

- Have you used that for a long time? He finally asked.

"Yes, " Lidia murmured, twisting the needle into a seizure. Nébel looked at her still and shrugged. However, as the mother repeated her injections with terrible frequency to drown out the pains of her kidney that the morphine had finished killing, Nébel decided to try the salvation of that wretch, stealing the drug from her.

-Octavio! Is going to kill me! She cried with a hoarse plea . My son Octavio!

I could not live a day!

- It is that it will not live two hours, if I leave that to him! -Nébel replied.

-It does not matter, my Octavio! Give me, give me morphine!

Nébel let the arms lie to him uselessly, and left with Lydia.

- Do you know the seriousness of your mother's condition? -Yes ... The doctors had told me ...

He stared at her.

-It is much worse than you imagine. Lydia went white, and looking outside she choked a sob bit her lips.

- There is no doctor here? He murmured.

"Not here, not in ten leagues around; but we will search.

That afternoon the mail arrived when they were alone in the dining room, and Nébel opened a letter.

-News? Lidia asked uneasily, raising her eyes to him. Quiet your eyes to the...

"Yes , " said Nébel, continuing the reading.

-The doctor? Lidia returned after a while, even more anxious.

"No, my wife, " he said in a hard voice, not raising his eyes. At ten o'clock at night, Lidia came running to the room of Nébel.

-Octavio! Mom dies! ...

They ran to the sick woman's room. An intense pallor was already covering the face. His lips were enormously swollen and blue, and between them escaped a word imitation, guttural and mouth full:

-Pla ... pla ... pla ...

Nébel saw at once on the night table the bottle of morphine, almost empty.

- It's clear, he's dying! Who gave you this? -I ask

-I do not know, Octavio! A while ago I heard noise ... Surely I went to look for your room when you were not ... Mom, poor mom! -He sobbed on the miserable arm that hung to the floor.

Nébel pushed it; the heart did not give anymore, and the temperature dropped. After a while the lips shut up their pla ... and on the skin appeared large violet spots.

At one in the morning he died. That afternoon, after the funeral, Nébel waited for Lidia to finish dressing while the peons loaded the suitcases in the carriage.

"Take this, " he said when she was beside him, handing him a check for ten thousand pesos. Lydia shuddered violently, and her red eyes fixed squarely on Nebel's. But he held his gaze.

-*Tonta*, then! He repeated surprised.

Lidia took it and went down to pick up her suitcase. Nébel then bent over she.

" Forgive me, " he said . Do not judge me worse than I am. At the station they waited a while and without speaking, next to the carriageway ladder, because the train was not leaving yet. When the bell rang, Lidia held out her hand, which Nébel held for a moment in silence. Then, without letting go, he picked Lidia up by the waist and kissed her deeply on the mouth.

The train left. Immobile, Nébel followed with her eyes the window that was lost. But Lidia did not show up.

THE DEATH OF ISOLDA

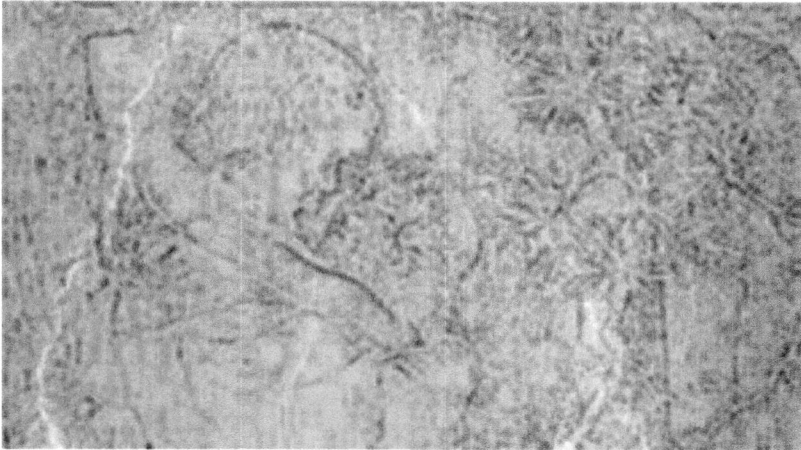

The first act of Tristan and Isolde was concluded . Tired of the turmoil of that day, I stayed in my chair, very happy with my loneliness. I turned my head to the living room, and immediately stopped my eyes in a low box.

Obviously, a marriage. He, any husband, and perhaps for his mercantile vulgarity and the difference of years with his wife, less than anyone.

She, young, pale, with one of those deep beauties that more than in the face – even beautiful -, resides in the perfect solidarity of look, mouth, neck, way of squinting. It was, above all, a beauty for men, without being in the least provocative; and this is precisely what women will never understand.

I stared at her for a long time because I saw her very well, and because when a man is thus tense to aspire to a beautiful body, he does not resort to the feminine discretion of glasses.

The second act began. I turned my head still to the box, and our eyes met. I, who had already appreciated the charm of that look wandering from one side of the room to the other, lived in a second, feeling it directly resting on me, the most adorable dream of love I have ever had.

That was very quick: the eyes fled, but two or three times, in my long minute of insistence, they turned briefly to me.

It was also, with the sudden happiness of having dreamed for a moment of her husband, the quickest disenchantment of an idyll. His eyes came back again, but at that moment I felt that my neighbor on the left was looking there, and after a moment of immobility on both sides, they greeted each other.

So, I did not have the most remote right to consider myself a happy man, and I observed my partner. He was a man of more than thirty-five years of age, with a blond beard and blue eyes with a clear and somewhat harsh look, which expressed an unequivocal will.

"They know each other, " I told myself, " and not a little. In effect, after half of the act my neighbor, who had not turned his eyes away from the scene,

fixed them in the box. She, her head a little back and in the gloom, looked at him too. It seemed even paler to me. They stared at each other, insistently, isolated from the world in that parallel line from soul to soul that kept them immobile.

During the third, my neighbor did not turn his head for a moment. But before concluding that one, it left by the lateral corridor. I looked at the box, and she had also retired.

"End of idyll, " I said melancholy. He did not come back, and the box was empty.

...

"Yes, they repeat themselves." He shook his head for a long time . All dramatic situations can be repeated, even the most unlikely, and repeated. It is necessary to live, and you are very young ... And those of your Tristan too, what does not stop there is the most sustained scream of passion that the human soul has cried out ... I love you as much as you do that work, and maybe more ... I do not mean, you'll want to believe, to Tristan's drama , and with it the thirty-six situations of dogma, out of which all are repetitions. Do not; the scene that returns like a nightmare, the characters that suffer the hallucination of dead happiness, is another thing ... You attended the prelude to one of those repetitions ... Yes, I know you remember ... We did not know each other with you then ... And ... precisely you should tell her about this! But he misjudges what he saw and believed a happy act of mine ... Happy! ...

Hear me The ship leaves in a moment, and this time I will not be back ...

I tell this to you, as if you could write it, for two reasons: First, because you have a striking resemblance to what I was then - in the good only, luckily -. And second, because you, my young friend, are perfectly incapable of pretending it, after what you are going to hear. Hear me:

I met her ten years ago, and during the six months that I was her boyfriend I did what was in me to be mine. He loved her very much, and she, immensely my. That is why it gave way one day, and from that moment my love, deprived of tension, cooled down.

Our social environment was different, and while she got drunk with the happiness of owning my name, I lived in a world sphere where it was inevitable to flirt with girls with surnames, fortune, and sometimes very pretty.

One of them took with me the flirting under garden party parasols to such an extreme that I became exasperated and pretended it seriously. But if my person was interesting for those games, my fortune was not enough to promise him the necessary train, and he made it clear to me.

He was right, perfect reason. Consequently flirted with a friend of his, much uglier, but infinitely less skillful for these tortures of *tete* -a- ten inches, whose exclusive grace is to drive your flirt crazy, keeping one owner of himself. And this time it was not me who got exasperated.

Surely, then, of the triumph, I thought then of the way to break with Ines. I continued to see her, and although she could not deceive herself about the deadening of my passion, her love was too great not to illuminate her eyes with happiness every time she saw me arrive.

The mother left us alone; and even if he had known what was happening, he would have closed his eyes so as not to lose the vaguest possibility of going up with his daughter to a much higher sphere.

One night I went there ready to break, with visible bad mood, for the same reason.

Agnes ran to hug me, but stopped, abruptly pale.

-What do you have? -he told me.

"Nothing, " I replied with a forced smile, stroking his forehead. She left to do, without paying attention to my hand and looking at me insistently. At last he turned his eyes away and we entered the room.

The mother came, but feeling a storm sky, she was only a moment and disappeared.

Breaking is short and easy word; but start it ...

We had sat down and we were not talking. Ines leaned forward, pushed my hand away from her face and stabbed at my eyes, painful with anguished examination.

- It is evident! ... - it murmured.

-What? I asked coldly.

The tranquility of my eyes hurt him more than my voice, and his face was changed:

-You do not love me anymore! He articulated in a desperate and slow swing of his head.

"This is the fiftieth time you say the same thing, " I answered.

There could be no harsher response; but I already had the beginning.

Ines looked at me for a while almost like a stranger, and brusquely pushing my hand away with her cigar, her voice broke:

-Esteban!

-What? -*Torné* to repeat.

This time was enough. He slowly put my hand down and leaned back on the sofa, keeping his livid face fixed on the lamp. But a moment later his face fell sideways under the twisted arm of the backrest.

It still happened a while. The injustice of my attitude-I saw only injustice in it -added to my deep self-disgust. That's why when I heard, or rather felt, that the tears were finally coming up, I got up with a violent snap of my tongue.

- I thought that we were not going to have more scenes - I said walking around. He did not answer me, and I added:

-But this is the last one.

I felt the tears stop, and under them I answered a moment later:

-As you like.

But then he fell sobbing on the couch:

-But what have I done to you! What did I do to you!

-Nothing! I replied . But I have not done anything to you either ... I think we're in the same case I'm sick of these things!

My voice was surely much harder than my words. Ines sat up, and holding on to the arm of the sofa, she repeated, frozen:

-As you like.

It was a farewell. I was going to break, and they were ahead of me. Self-love, vile self-love touched alive, made me respond.

-Perfectly ... I'm leaving. May you be happier ... again.

He did not understand, and he looked at me strangely. I had already committed the first infamy: and as in those cases, I felt the vertigo of getting even more muddy.

-Is clear! -I supported brutally . Because you have not had a complaint about me, right? ... do not?

I mean, I did the honor of being your lover, and you should be grateful. He understood my smile more than my words, and while I went looking for my hat in the corridor, his body and his whole soul collapsed in the room.

Then, in that moment when I crossed the gallery, I felt intensely what I had just done. Luxury aspiration, lofty marriage, everything highlighted me as a wound in my own soul. And I, who offered me at auction the ugly mundane with fortune, who put me on sale, had just committed the most outrageous act, with the woman who loved us too much ... *Skinnyness* on the Mount of

Olives, or moment vile in a man who is not, they lead to the same end: desire for sacrifice, for a higher reconquest of one's worth. And then, the immense thirst for tenderness, to erase kiss after kiss the tears of the adored woman, whose first smile after the wound we have caused her, is the most beautiful light that can flood a man's heart.

And concluded! It was not possible for me to take back what I had just insulted in that way: I was no longer worthy of it, I deserved it no more. He had muddied in a second the purest love that any man had felt about himself, and had just lost with Ines the irreducible happiness of possessing the one who loves us dearly.

Desperate, humiliated, I crossed in front of the room, and saw her lying on the sofa, sobbing the whole soul in her arms.

Agnes! Lost already! I felt deeper my misery before his body, all love, shaken by the sobs of his dead happiness. Almost without noticing, I stopped.

-Agnes! -said.

My voice was not the same as before. And she must have felt it, because her soul felt, in sobs, the desperate call that my love made to her - that time, yes, immense love!

-No, no ... -he replied -. It's too late!...

Padilla stopped. I have seldom seen bitterness more dry and calm than that of his eyes when he finished. For my part, I could not remove from my memory that adorable beauty of the box, sobbing on the sofa ...

"I will believe," Padilla said, "if I tell him that in my insomnia as a single unhappy man I have had it before me ... I left Buenos Aires without seeing almost anyone, especially my flirt of great fortune. I returned at the age of eight, and I knew then that he had married, six months after I left. I turned away, and a month ago I returned, well reassured, and in peace. He had not seen her again. It was for me like a first love, with all the dignifying charm that a virginal idyll has for man-made that he loved a hundred times later ... If you are ever loved as I was, and outraged as I did, you will understand all the purity that is in my memory.

Until one night I ran into her. Yes, that same night in the theater ... I understood, seeing the opulent grocer of her husband, who had rushed into marriage, as I did the Ucayali ... But seeing her again, twenty meters from me, watching me , I felt that in my soul, asleep in peace, I was bleeding out of the desolation of having lost her, as if one day of those ten years had not passed.

Agnes! Her beauty, her look - unique among all the women - had been mine, well mine, because she had been given to me with adoration. You will also appreciate this one day.

I did what was humanly possible to forget, I broke my teeth trying to concentrate all my thoughts on the scene. But the prodigious score of Wagner, that cry of sickening passion, ignited in a living flame what he wanted to forget. In the second or third act I could not take it anymore and I turned my head. She also suffered Wagner's suggestion, and looked at me. Agnes, my life!

For half a minute her mouth, her hands, were under my mouth and my eyes, and during that time she concentrated in her pallor the sensation of that dead happiness ten years ago. And always, Tristan , his screams

of superhuman passion, about our happiness !

I got up then, crossed the seats like a sleepwalker, and walked down the hall approaching her without seeing her, without seeing me, as if for ten years I had not been a miserable ...

And like ten years ago, I suffered the hallucination that I was holding my hat in my hand and was going to pass in front of her.

I passed, the door to the box was open, and I stopped crazily. As ten years before on the sofa, she, Agnes, now stretched out on the divan in the ante-pillar, sobbed Wagner's passion and her unraveling happiness.

Inés! ... I felt that destiny put me in a decisive moment. Ten years! ... But had they happened? No, not Agnes mine!

And as then, seeing her body all love, shaken by sobs, I called her:

-Agnes!

And like ten years before, the sobs redoubled, and as then he answered me under his arms:

-No, no ... It's too late!

A LONELY MAN

Kassim was a sickly man, a jeweler by trade, well he had no established shop. He worked for large houses, his specialty being the assembly of precious stones. Few hands like yours for delicate settings. With more boot and commercial skill he would have been rich. But at thirty-five, she continued in her room, dressed in a workshop under the window.

Kassim, with a petty body, a bloodless face shaded by a thin black beard, had a beautiful and strongly passionate woman. The young woman, of street origin, had aspired with her beauty to a higher bond. He waited until he was twenty, provoking the men and their neighbors with his body. Fearful at last, she accepted Kassim nervously.

No more luxury dreams, however. Her husband, a skilled artist-still, was completely lacking in character to make a fortune. Therefore, while the jeweler was working folded on her tweezers, she, with her elbows, was holding a slow and heavy gaze on her husband, then abruptly tearing herself away and continuing with her eyes behind the glass to the passer-by who could have been her husband .

How much Kassim earned, however, was for her. On Sundays he also worked so that he could offer him a supplement. When Maria wanted a jewel - and with what passion she wanted!

-He worked at night. Afterwards there were coughs and stitches at the side; but Maria had her sparks of brilliance.

Little by little the daily treatment with the gems came to make the wife love the tasks of the architect, following with ardent ardor the intimate delicacies of the setting. But when the jewel was finished - she must leave, it was not for her - she fell more deeply into the disappointment of her marriage. The jewel was tested, stopping before the mirror. At last he left her there, and went to his room.

Kassim woke up when he heard her sobs, and found her in bed, not wanting to hear him.

"I do, however, as much as I can for you, " he said at last, sadly.

The sobs went up with this, and the jeweler slowly reinstalled himself in his bank.

These things were repeated, so much so that Kassim did not get up to comfort her.

Comforting her! Of what? This did not prevent Kassim from prolonging his evenings in order to get a bigger supplement.

He was an indecisive man, irresolute and quiet. His wife's eyes now stopped with a heavier fixity on that silent tranquility.

-And you are a man, you! He murmured. Kassim, on his links, did not stop moving his fingers.

"You're not happy with me, Maria," he said after a while.

-Happy! And you have the courage to say it! Who can be happy with you? ... Not the last of the women! ... Poor devil! -Concluding with nervous laughter, leaving.

Kassim worked that night until three o'clock in the morning, and his wife then had new sparks that she considered for a moment with tight lips.

-Yes ... It's not a surprising diadem ... When did you do it?

"Since Tuesday, " he said with faded tenderness ; while you were Sleeping,

at night...

-Oh, you could have slept! ... Immense, the brilliant ones!

Because his passion was the voluminous stones that Kassim rode. He continued the work with mad hunger that would end at once, and as soon as he dressed the jewel, he would run with it to the mirror. Then, a sob attack:

-All, any husband, the last, would make a sacrifice to flatter his wife! And you ... and you ...

Not a miserable dress to wear!

When a certain limit of respect for the male is transferred, the woman can get to tell her husband incredible things.

Kassim's wife crossed that line with a passion equal to at least that of the brilliant. One afternoon, while keeping his jewelry, Kassim noticed the lack of a pin - five thousand pesos in two solitaires -. He looked in his drawers again.

- You have not seen the pin, Maria? I left it here.

-Yes I saw it.

-Where is? -He turned surprised.

-Here!

His wife, her eyes alight and her mouth mocking, stood with the pin on.

"It suits you very well, " said Kassim after a while . Let's keep it.

Maria laughed.

-Oh no! It's mine.

-Joke?...

-Yes, it's a joke! Just kidding, yes! How it hurts to think that it could be mine ...! Tomorrow I

will give it to you. Today I go to the theater with him.

Kassim was demure.

-You do wrong ... They could see you. They would lose all confidence in me.

-Oh! She closed with furious annoyance, thumping the door violently. Returning from the theater, he placed the jewel on the table. Kassim got up from the bed and went to keep it in his workshop under lock and key. When he returned, his wife was sitting on the bed.

- That is to say, you are afraid that I will steal it! That I am a thief!

-Don't look like that ... You've been reckless, nothing more.

-Ah! And they entrust it to you! To you, to you! And when your wife asks for a little flattery, and she wants ...! You call me a thief, you infamous!

He fell asleep at last. But Kassim did not sleep.

They then gave Kassim to ride, a loner, the most admirable brilliant that would have passed through his hands.

-Look, Maria, what a rock. I have not seen another like it. His wife said nothing; but Kassim felt her breathing deeply over the lonely man.

"Wonderful water ... " he continued . It will cost nine or ten thousand pesos.

"A ring ... " Maria murmured at last.

-No, it's a man's ... A pin.

In time with the assembly of the solitary, Kassim received on his working back all that burned with resentment and frustrated cooting in his wife. Ten times a day she interrupted her husband to go with the bright one in front of the mirror. Then I tried it with different dresses.

"If you want to do it later, " Kassim dared one day . It is an urgent job. He waited in vain; his wife opened the balcony.

-María, they can see you!

-Taking! There is your stone!

The solitary, violently torn from the neck, rolled across the floor.

Kassim, livid, picked it up, examined it and then raised his gaze from his wife to the ground.

-And well: Why do you look at me like that? Did your stone do something?

"No , " said Kassim. And immediately he resumed his task, although his hands trembled to pity.

He had to get up at last to see his wife in the bedroom, in the middle of a nervous breakdown. Her hair had come loose, and her eyes were coming out of their sockets.

-Give to me the sparkly! He cried . Give it to me! We will escape! For me!

Give it to me!

"Maria ... " Kassim stammered, trying to get rid of himself.

-Ah! Roared his crazed wife . You are the thief, miserable! You have stolen my life, thief, thief!

And you thought I was not going to retaliate ... cuckold! AHA! Look at me. It never occurred to you, huh? Oh! -And took both hands to the throat drowned. But when Kassim left, he jumped out of bed and fell to his chest, reaching for a booty.

-No matter! The bright one, give it to me! I do not want more than that! It's mine, Kassim miserable!

Kassim helped her up, livid.
-You're sick, Maria. Then we'll talk about it...
Lay down.
-My brilliant!
-Well, we'll see if it's possible ... Go to bed.
-Give it to me!
The nervous crisis returned.

Kassim went back to work on his solitaire. Since his hands had a mathematical certainty, few were missing a few hours before concluding it.

Maria got up to eat, and Kassim had the usual request with her. At the end of the dinner his wife looked at him straight ahead.
"It's a lie, Kassim, " he said.
-Oh! Kassim replied smiling . Is nothing.
-I swear it's a lie! She insisted.

Kassim smiled again, touching his hand with a clumsy caress, and got up to continue his work. His wife, with her cheeks in her hands, followed him with her eyes.

"And he does not tell me more than that ... " he murmured. And with a deep nausea that sticky, flabby and inert that was her husband, went to his room.

He did not sleep well. He woke up, late, and saw light in the workshop; her husband continued working. An hour later Kassim heard a scream.
-Give it to me!
-Yes it's for you; Little is missing, Maria, "he said hurriedly, getting up. But his wife, after that cry of nightmare, slept again.

At two o'clock in the morning Kassim was able to finish his task: the brilliant shone firm and manly in its setting. With a silent step he went to the bedroom and lit the candle. Maria slept on her back, in the frozen whiteness of her chest and her nightgown.

He went to the workshop and came back again. He looked for a while at the almost bare breast, and with a faded smile he pushed the loose gown a little further away. His wife did not feel it.

There was not much light. Kassim's face suddenly acquired a hardness of stone, and suspending for a moment the jewel in flower of the naked breast, he sank, firm and perpendicular as a nail, the whole pin in the heart of his wife.

There was a sharp opening of eyes, followed by a slow drop of eyelids. The fingers arched, and nothing else.

The jewel, shaken by the convulsion of the injured ganglion, shook an unbalanced moment. Kassim waited a moment; and when the solitary was finally perfectly immobile, he withdrew, closing the door behind him without making a sound.

SUICIDING SHIPS

It turns out that there are few things more terrible than finding an abandoned ship in the sea.

If by day the danger is less, at night the ship is not seen nor is there any possible warning: the collision is carried to one and the other.

These ships abandoned by year or by year, sail stubbornly in favor of currents or wind; if they have the sails deployed. They travel like this the seas, changing capriciously of course.

Not a few of the steamers that one day did not reach port, have stumbled on their way with one of these silent ships that travel on their own. There is always a chance to find them, every minute. By chance the currents tend to entangle them in the seas of *sargasso*. The ships stop, finally, here or there, immobile forever in that desert of seaweed. So, until little by little they are falling apart. But others arrive every day, occupy their place in silence, so that the quiet and gloomy port is always frequented.

The main reason for these ship abandonments are undoubtedly the storms and fires that leave black roving skeletons. But there are other singular causes among which one can include what happened to María Margarita , who sailed from New York on August 24, 1903, and that on the morning of the 26th she spoke with a corvette, without accusing any novelty. Four hours later, a package, not getting an answer, detached a boat that boarded María Margarita . There was no one on the ship. The sailors' shirts were drying in the bow. The kitchen was still on. A sewing machine had the needle suspended over the seam, as if it had been left a moment before. There was no sign of struggle or panic, all in perfect order. And all were missing. What happened?

The night I learned this we were gathered on the bridge. We were going to Europe, and the captain told us his marine history, perfectly true, on the other hand.

The female crowd, won by the suggestion of whispering waves, heard shuddering. The nervous girls lent an uneasy ear to the husky voice of the sailors in the bow. A very young and newly married lady dared:

- They will not be eagles ...?

The captain smiled kindly:

- What, ma'am? Eagles take the crew? Everyone laughed, and the girl did the same, a little cut.

Happily, a passenger knew something of that. We look at it curiously. During the trip he had been an excellent companion, admiring at his own risk, and speaking little.

-Ah! If he told us, sir! The young girl with the eagles pleaded.

"I have no problem ," the discreet individual agreed . In two words: in the northern seas, like the captain's Maria Margaret , we once found a sailing ship. Our course - we were also sailing -,

took us almost to his side. The singular air of abandonment that does not cheat on a ship caught our attention, and we slowed down observing it. At last we took off a boat; On board no one was found, everything was also in perfect order. But the last entry in the diary was four days ago, so we do not feel much of an impression. We still laugh a little about the famous sudden disappearances.

Eight of our men remained on board for the government of the new ship. We would travel in preserve. At nightfall he took us a little way. The next day we reached it, but we did not see anyone on the bridge. The sloop again broke off, and those who went in vain crossed the ship: all had disappeared. Not an object out of its place. The sea was absolutely smooth throughout. A pot of potatoes still boiled in the kitchen.

As you will understand, the superstitious terror of our people reached its height. In the long run, six were encouraged to fill the void, and I went with them. Hardly on board, my new companions decided to drink to banish all worry. They were sitting in a wheel, and by the time most were singing.

He arrived midday and took a nap. At four o'clock, the breeze stopped and the candles fell. A sailor approached the rail and looked at the oily sea. Everyone had gotten up, pacing, not wanting to talk anymore. One sat on a rolled rope and took off his shirt to patch it up. He sewed a while in silence. Suddenly he got up and let out a long whistle. His companions turned. He looked at them vaguely, surprised too, and sat down again. A moment later he left the shirt on the roll, advanced to the rail and threw himself into the water. When they heard noise, the others turned their heads, frowning slightly. But they soon seemed to forget about the incident, returning to common apathy.

After a while another stretched, rubbed his eyes walking, and threw himself into the water.

Half an hour passed; the sun was falling. I felt suddenly that they touched me on the shoulder.

-What time is it?

"Five o'clock, " I replied. The old sailor who had asked me the question looked at me distrustfully, with his hands in his pockets. He looked at my pants for a long time, distracted. At last he threw himself into the water.

The three that remained, approached quickly and observed the whirlpool. They sat on the rail, whistling slowly, their eyes lost in the distance. One got out and lay down on the bridge, tired.

The others disappeared one after the other. At six o'clock, the last of them all got up, composed his clothes, brushed his hair back from his forehead, walked still sleepy, and threw himself into the water.

Then I was alone, looking like an idiot the deserted sea. All without knowing what they were doing, they had thrown themselves into the sea, wrapped in the sleepy somnambulism that floated on the ship. When one was thrown into the water, the others became momentarily worried, as if remembering something, to forget immediately. That was how they had disappeared, and I suppose the same as those of the previous day, and the others and those of the other ships. This is all.

We stare at the weird man with explainable curiosity.

- And you did not feel anything? -Asked my

- Yes; a great reluctance and obstinacy of the same ideas, but nothing more. I do not know why I did not feel anything else. I presume that the reason is this: instead of to exhaust myself in an anguished defense and at all costs against what I felt, as all must have done, and even the sailors without realizing it, I simply accepted that hypnotic death, as if it were already annulled. Something very similar has undoubtedly happened to the sentinels of that famous guard, who hanged themselves night after night.

As the comment was quite complicated, no one responded. Shortly after the narrator retired to his cabin. The captain followed him for a while.

-Phony! He murmured.

"On the contrary, " said a sick passenger, who was going to die to his land . If he were a phony, he would not have stopped thinking about that, and he would have thrown himself into the water too.

ADRIFT

The man stepped on something soft, and immediately felt the bite on his foot. He leapt forward, and when he turned with an oath he saw a *yararacusu* that, overwhelmed by itself, awaited another attack.

The man glanced quickly at his foot, where two droplets of blood thickened, and the machete drew blood from his waist. The snake saw the threat, and sank its head deeper into the center of its spiral; but the machete fell on its back, dislocating its vertebrae.

The man climbed down to the bite, removed the droplets of blood, and for a moment I watched. A sharp pain arose from the two violet spots, and began to invade the entire foot.

Hurriedly he tied his ankle with his handkerchief, and followed the chop to his ranch.

The pain in the foot increased, with a sensation of tight bulge, and suddenly the man felt two or three flashing stitches that like lightning had radiated from the wound to the middle of the calf.

He moved his leg with difficulty; A metallic dryness of throat, followed by burning thirst, took a new oath.

He finally arrived at the ranch, and threw himself on the wheel of a sugar mill. The two violet dots were now disappearing into the monstrous swelling of the entire foot. The skin seemed thin and ready to give way, tense. The man wanted to call his wife, and the voice broke in a hoarse drag of a parched throat. Thirst devoured him.

-Dorotea! He managed to throw in a rattle . Give cane!

His wife ran with a full glass, which the man sipped in three gulps. But I did not enjoy it at all.

-I asked you cane, not water! He roared again . Give cane! - But it is cane, Paulino! Protested the frightened woman. -No, you gave me water!

I want cane, I tell you!

The woman ran again, returning with the demijohn. The man swallowed two glasses one after the other, but he felt nothing in his throat.

-Good; this is ugly ... "he murmured then, looking at his livid foot and already with gangrenous luster. On the deep tie of the handkerchief, the flesh overflowed like a monstrous blood sausage.

The shining pains followed one another in continuous flashes, and now reached the groin.

The excruciating dryness of the throat that the breath seemed to warm more, increased at the same time. When he tried to sit up, a fulminating vomit kept him half a minute with his forehead resting on the wooden wheel.

But the man did not want to die, and descending to the coast he climbed into his canoe. He sat in the stern and began to paddle to the center of Paraná. There the current of the river, which in the vicinity of the Iguazú runs six miles, would take it before five hours to Tacurú -Pucú.

The man, with somber energy, was able to reach the middle of the river; but there his sleeping hands dropped the shovel in the canoe, and after a new vomit -of blood this time —he looked at the sun that was already transposing the mountain.

The entire leg, up to half a thigh, was already a deformed and very hard block that burst the clothes. The man cut the ligature and opened the pants with his knife: the lower belly overflowed swollen, with large livid spots and terribly painful. The man thought that he would never be able to reach Tacurú on his own - Lucía, and he decided to ask his compadre Alves for help, although they had been displeased for a long time.

The current of the river was now rushing towards the Brazilian coast, and the man could easily dock. He crawled up the hill, but at twenty meters, exhausted, he lay on his chest.

- Alves! He cried as loudly as he could; and he listened in vain.

-*Compadre Alves*! Do not deny me this favor! He cried again, raising his head from the ground. In the silence of the forest there was not a single rumor. The man still had courage to reach his canoe, and the current, catching it again, took it swiftly adrift. The Paraná runs there at the bottom of an immense basin, whose walls, high of one hundred meters, coffin the river. From the banks bordered by black blocks of basalt ascends the forest, black as well. Forward, to the sides, behind, always the eternal lugubrious wall, in whose bottom the swirling river rushes in incessant bursts of muddy water. The landscape is aggressive, and there reigns in it a silence of death. At sunset, however, its *sombre* and calm beauty takes on a unique majesty.

The sun had already fallen when the man, lying at the bottom of the canoe, had a violent chill. And suddenly, with astonishment, he lifted his head heavily: he felt better. His leg hurt slightly, his thirst abated, and his chest, free now, opened in slow inspiration.

The poison began to leave, there was no doubt. He was almost well, and although he did not have the strength to move his hand, he counted on the fall of the dew to recover completely.

He calculated that before three hours he would be in Tacurú -Pucú.

Welfare progressed and with it a drowsiness full of memories. I did not feel anything in my leg or belly anymore. Would his compadre Gaona still live in Tacurú -Pucú? Perhaps he also saw his former employer, Mr. Dougald, and the recipient of the work.

Would he arrive soon? The sky, to the west, now opened on a golden screen, and the river had also colored. From the Paraguayan coast, already darkened, the mountain let fall on the river its crepuscular freshness, in penetrating effluvia of orange blossom and wild honey. A pair of macaws crossed very loudly and silently towards Paraguay.

Down below, on the river of gold, the canoe drifted swiftly, turning at times on itself before the bubbling of a whirlpool. The man who went there felt better and better, and thought in the meantime about the exact time he had spent without seeing his ex-patron Dougald. Three years? Maybe not, not so much. Two years and nine months? Perhaps. Eight and a half months? Of course, surely.

Suddenly he felt that he was frozen to the chest. It would? And the breathing...

At the wooden hall of Mr. Dougald, Lorenzo Cubilla, he had known in Puerto Esperanza on a Good Friday ... Friday? Yes, or Thursday ...

The man slowly stretched his fingers.

-A thursday...

And stopped breathing.

THE INSOLATION

Old puppy went out the door and crossed the yard with a straight and lazy step. He stopped at the edge of the grass, stretched to the mountain, squinting, vibrating nose, and sat quietly. I saw the monotonous plain of the Chaco, with its alternatives of field and mountain, mountain and field, with no more color than the cream of the grass and the black of the mountain. This closed the horizon, two hundred meters, on three sides of the farm. To the west, the field widened and spread out in the open, but the inescapable dark line framed in the distance.

At that early hour, the border, obfuscating light at noon, acquired a sharp clarity. There was not a cloud nor a breath of wind. Under the calm of the silvery sky, the field exuded a cool freshness that brought the thoughtful soul, before the certainty of another dry day, melancholy of better compensated work.

Milk, the puppy's father, crossed the yard in turn and sat next to him, with a lazy moan of well-being. Both remained motionless, because there were no flies yet.

Old, who had been looking for a while at the mountain side, observed:

-The morning is cool.

Milk followed the puppy's gaze and stared, blinking absentmindedly. After a while he said:

-In that tree there are two hawks.

They returned the indifferent sight to an ox that passed, and they continued watching by habit the things.

Meanwhile, the east began to fan out, and the horizon had already lost its morning precision.

Milk crossed his front legs and in doing so felt slight pain. He looked at his fingers without moving, finally deciding to sniff them. The previous day he had taken a pique, and in memory of what he had suffered he licked extensively the diseased finger.

"I could not walk, " he said in conclusion. -Old did not understand what he meant, Milk added: -There are many piques.

This time the puppy understood. And he replaced on his own, after long little while:

-There are many piques.

One and another fell silent again, convinced.

The sun came out; and in the first bath of his light, the turkeys of the mountain threw to the pure air the tumultuous trumpeting of his *charanga*. The dogs, golden in the oblique sun, narrowed their eyes, sweetening their softness in blessed blinking. Little by little the couple increased with the arrival of the other companions: Dick, the favorite taciturn; Prince, whose upper lip split by a coati, showed his teeth; and *Isondú*, of indigenous name. The five fox-terriers, lying down and blessed with well-being, slept.

After an hour they raised their heads; on the opposite side of the bizarre two-story ranch —the lower mud and the tall wood, with corridors and the railing of a chalet -they had felt the steps of their owner who descended the stairs. Mr. Jones, the towel on his shoulder, stopped for a moment in the corner of the ranch and looked at the sun, already high. He still had the dead look and the lip hanging behind his lonely evening of whiskey, longer than usual.

While he washed, the dogs came and sniffed at his boots, his tail bobbing lazily. Like the trained beasts, dogs know the least hint of drunkenness in their master. They moved slowly away to lie back in the sun. But the growing heat soon made them leave, through the shadow of the corridors.

The day progressed equal to the precedents of that month; dry, limpid, with fourteen hours of scorching sun that seemed to keep the sky in fusion, and that in an instant cracked the earth wet in blanquecinas crusts. Mr. Jones went to the farm, looked at the work of the previous day and returned to the ranch. In all that morning he did nothing. He had lunch and went up to nap.

The pawns returned to the two to the carpición, notwithstanding the hour of fire, because the weeds did not leave the cotton field. After them were the dogs, very close friends of the crop since last winter, when they learned to dispute the hawks the white worms that lifted the plow. Each dog was thrown under a cotton tree, accompanying with its panting the dull thuds of the hoe.

Meanwhile the heat grew. In the silent and blinding landscape of the sun, the air vibrated everywhere, damaging the view. The removed earth exhaled furnace vapor, which the peons endured on the head, wrapped up to the ears in the floating handkerchief, with the silence of their farm work. The dogs changed every moment of plant, in search of more cool shade. They stretched along, but fatigue forced them to sit on their hind legs to breathe better.

A small moorland that had not even tried to plow was now reverberating before them. There, the puppy suddenly saw Mr. Jones sitting on a log, which was staring at him. Old stood up, wagging his tail. The others stood up too, but bristled.

"It's the boss, " said the puppy, surprised at their attitude.

"No, it's not him, " said Dick.

The four dogs were huddled together growling deafly, without taking their eyes from Mr. Jones, who remained motionless, watching them. The puppy, incredulous, went forward, but Prince showed him his teeth:

-It's not him, it's Death.

The puppy bristled with fear and stepped back into the group.

- Is the pattern dead? He asked anxiously.

The others, without answering him, broke into barking with fury, always in an attitude of fearful attitude. But Mr. Jones was already vanishing in the undulating air.

When he heard barks, the pawns had looked up, not seeing anything. They turned their heads to see if any horses had entered the farm, and they bent again.

The fox- terriers returned to the ranch. The puppy, still bristling, came forward and back with short nervous trots, and learned from the experience of his companions that when a thing is going to die, appears earlier.

- And how do you know that the one we saw was not the living patron? - I ask.

-Because it was not him -they responded cavalierly.

Then Death, and with it the change of owner, the miseries, the kicks, was upon them! They spent the rest of the afternoon with their employer, somber and alert. At the slightest noise they growled, not knowing where.

At last the sun sank behind the black palm of the stream, and in the calm of the silver night, the dogs parked around the ranch, on whose high floor Mr. Jones began his evening of whiskey.

At midnight they heard his footsteps, then the fall of his boots on the plank floor, and the light went out. The dogs, then, felt more the next change of owner, and alone, at the foot of the sleeping house, they began to cry. They wept in chorus, turning their convulsive and dry sobs, as chewed, in a howl of desolation, which the voice of Prince's hunter held, while the others took the sob again. The puppy could only bark. The night was advancing, and the four old dogs, grouped in the moonlight, the muzzle extended and swollen with laments -Well fed and caressed by the owner they were going to lose- , they continued to cry at the top of their domestic misery.

The next morning Mr. Jones went himself to look for the mules and he joined them to the carpidora, working until nine o'clock. I was not satisfied, however. Apart from the fact that the earth had never been well traced, the blades had no edge, and with the rapid pace of the mules, the carpidora jumped. He returned with it and sharpened its bars; but a screw in which already when buying the machine had noticed a fault, broke when assembling it. He sent a pawn to the nearby obraje, recommending that he take care of the horse, a good animal but sunny. He raised his head to the midday sun, and insisted that he galloped for a moment. He had lunch right away and went upstairs. The dogs, who in the morning had not left a second to their employer, stayed in the corridors.

The siesta weighed, overwhelmed with light and silence. The whole outline was foggy from the burning. Around the ranch, the whitish ground of the patio dazzled the sun, seemed to deform in a trembling boil, numbing the blinking eyes of the fox- terriers.

"He has not come back, " said Milk.

Old, when he appeared , raised his ears brightly. Prompted by the evocation, the puppy got up and barked, looking for what. After a while he fell silent, surrendering with his companions to his defensive fly hunt.

"It did not come anymore, " Isondú added.

"There was a lizard under the raigon," Prince recalled for the first time.

A hen, the beak open and the wings apart from the body, crossed the incandescent courtyard with its heavy trot of heat. Prince followed lazily with his eyes, and jumped up.

- It's coming again! -scream.

The horse on which the pawn had gone was advancing on the north side of the courtyard.

The dogs arched on their legs, barking furiously at the approaching Death. The horse walked with his head down, seemingly indecisive about the course he should follow. As he passed the ranch, he took a few steps toward the well, and gradually faded into the harsh light.

Mr. Jones went down: he was not sleepy. He was ready to continue the assembly of the carpidora, when he saw the pawn arrive on horseback unexpectedly. Despite his order, he had to have galloped to return at that hour. As soon as his mission was over, the poor horse, on whose flanks it was impossible to count the beats, trembled with his head down, and fell on his side. Mr. Jones sent to the farm, still hat and whip, the pawn not to throw if he continued to hear his jesuitical apology.

But the dogs were happy. Death, who was looking for his employer, had settled for the horse.

They felt happy, free of worry, and consequently prepared to go to the farm after the pawn, when they heard Mr. Jones yelling at him, asking for the screw. There was no screw: the warehouse was closed, the manager was sleeping, etc. Mr. Jones, without replying, picked up his helmet and left himself in search of the utensil.

He resisted the sun like a pawn, and the walk was wonderful against his bad mood.

The dogs went out with him, but they stopped in the shade of the first carob tree; way too hot. From there, firm on the legs, frown contracted and attentive, they watched their employer go away. At last the fear of loneliness was over, and with a trot trot followed him.

Mr. Jones got his screw and came back. To shorten the distance, of course, avoiding the dusty curve of the road, he went in a straight line to his farm. He came to the stream and went into the *pajonal*, the rain-fed *pajonal* del *Saladito*, which has grown, dried and sprouted since there is straw in the world, without knowing fire. The bushes, arched in a vault at chest height, intertwine in solid blocks. The task of crossing it, would be already with a fresh day, it was very hard at that time. Mr. Jones went through it, however, braking through the shivering and dusty straw through the mud that the floods left, drowned in fatigue and acrid vapors of nitrates.

He finally left and stopped at the edge; but it was impossible to remain still under that sun and that fatigue. He marched again. In the burning heat that was growing steadily from three days ago, the suffocation of decomposed time was now added. The sky was white and there was no breath of wind. The air was missing, with heart anguish that did not allow to finish the breathing.

Mr. Jones acquired the conviction that he had crossed his limit of resistance. For some time, the beat of the carotids had been pounding in his ears. He felt himself in the air, as if from inside his head they were pushing his skull upwards. It was marked by looking at the grass. He hurried the march to put an end to that at once ... And suddenly he came to himself and found himself in a different place: he had walked half a block without realizing anything. He looked back, and his head went into new vertigo.

In the meantime, the dogs followed him, trotting with all their tongues outside. Sometimes, asphyxiated, they stopped in the shade of a small knife; they sat precipitating their panting, to return at once to the torment of the sun. At last, as the house was already close, they hurried the trot.

It was at that moment that Old, who was ahead, saw behind the fence of the farm Mr. Jones, dressed in white, walking towards them. The puppy, with sudden memory, turned his head to his employer and confronted.

-The Death, the Death! He howled.

The others had seen it too, and barked bristling. They saw Mr. Jones go through the fence and for a moment they thought he was going to make a mistake; but when he reached a hundred meters he stopped, looked at the group with his celestial eyes, and marched forward.

- Do not walk the pattern lightly! Prince exclaimed. - He's going to trip over him! Everyone howled.

In effect, the other, after brief hesitation, had advanced, but not directly on them as before, but in an oblique and seemingly erroneous line, but which had to take him right to meet Mr. Jones. The dogs understood that this time everything was over, because their boss kept walking at the same pace, like an automaton, without noticing anything. The other was already there. The dogs dipped their tails and ran sideways, howling. A second passed, and the meeting occurred. Mr. Jones stopped, turned and collapsed.

The pawns, who saw him fall, hurried him to the ranch, but all the water was useless; He died without returning to himself. Mister Moore, his maternal brother, went there from Buenos Aires, spent an hour at the farm and in four days liquidated everything, immediately turning to the south. The Indians divided up the dogs, who lived in the front skinny and mangy, and went every night with hungry stealth to steal ears of corn in the fields of others.

THE WIRE OF PÚA

For fifteen days the sorrel horse had searched in vain for the path through which his companion was escaping from the paddock. The formidable fence, *capuera* - dismount that has regrown inextricable -, did not allow step even to the head of the horse. Evidently it was not around where the *malacara* passed.

The sorrel walked the farm again, trotting restlessly with his head alert. From the depth of the mountain, the *malacara* responded to the vibrating neighing of his companion with his short and quick ones, in which there was a fraternal promise of abundant food. The most irritating to the sorrel was that the *malacara* reappeared two or three times a day to drink. He promised himself then not to leave his companion for a moment, and for a few hours, in fact, the couple grazed in admirable preserves. But suddenly the *malacara*, with its rope dragged, went into the *chircal*, and when the sorrel, realizing his solitude, launched in pursuit, found the inextricable mount. This yes, from inside, very close still, the evil *malacara* responded to his desy neighs, with a neigh with full mouth.

Until that morning the old sorrel found the breach very simply: crossing in front of the chircal, which from the mountain advanced fifty meters in the field, he saw a vague path that led him in perfect oblique line to the mountain. There was the malacara, stripping trees.

The thing was very simple: the malacara, crossing the chircal one day, had found the gap opened in the mountain by an uprooted incense. He repeated his progress through the chircal, until he got to know perfectly the entrance of the tunnel. Then he used the old road that with the sorrel had formed along the line of the mountain. And here was the cause of the upheaval of the sorrel: the entrance of the path formed a very oblique line with the path of the horses, so that the sorrel, accustomed to traverse it from south to north and never from north to south, would not have never found the breach.

In an instant the old horse was joined to his companion, and together then, with no other concern than awkwardly popping the palms Young, the two horses decided to get away from the unfortunate pasture they already knew by heart.

The mountain, extremely thinned, allowed an easy advance, even to horses. Of the forest it was not really a strip of two hundred meters wide. Behind him, a two-year-old hood was plowing wild tobacco. The old sorrel, who in his youth had run around capueras until he had lived six months in them, led the way, and in half an hour the next cigars were left bare with leaves as far as a horse's neck.

Walking, eating, browsing, the sorrel and the malacara crossed the bonnet until a wire fence stopped them.

"A fence , " said the sorrel.

"Yes, wired." The malacha nodded. And both, passing their heads over the upper thread, contemplated attentively. From there one could see a high pasture of old grazed, white by the frost; a bananal and a new plantation. All this little tempting, no doubt; but the horses understood to see that, and one after another they followed the fence to the right.

Two minutes later they passed; a tree, standing dry by fire, had fallen on the threads. They crossed the whiteness of the frozen grass in which their footsteps did not sound, and skirting the red banana tree, burned by the frost, they then saw closely what these new plants were.

"It's yerba, " the malacara said, his tremulous lips half a centimeter from the hard leaves. The disappointment could have been great; but the horses, although greedy, aspired above all to walk.

So cutting obliquely the yerbal they continued their way, until a new fence contained the couple.

They took care of it with serious and patient tranquility, thus arriving at a gate, open for their happiness, and the passers-by suddenly saw themselves in the middle of the royal road.

Now, for the horses, what they had just done had all the appearance of a feat. From the boring pasture to the present freedom, there was infinite distance. But as infinite as it was, the horses intended to prolong it still, and so, after observing with lazy attention the surroundings, they took off mutually the dandruff of the neck, and in gentle happiness they continued their adventure.

The day, in truth, favored her. The morning mist of Misiones had just completely dissipated, and under the suddenly blue sky, the landscape shone with splendid clarity. From the hill whose summit the two horses occupied at that moment, the red dirt road cut the grass in front of them with admirable precision, descended to the white valley of icy espartillo, to go back up to the distant mountain. The wind, very cold, crystallized even more the clarity of the golden morning, and the horses, who felt the sun in front, almost horizontal still, squinted at the happy dazzle.

They continued like this, alone and glorious of freedom in the path lit with light, until when they turned a point of mount they saw on the side of the road a certain extension of an unusual green. Grass? Definitely. But in the middle of winter ...

And with dilated noses of gluttony, the horses approached the fence. Yes, fine grass, admirable grass! And they would enter, free horses!

It is necessary to notice that the sorrel and the malacara owned since that dawn high idea of themselves. Neither gate, nor fence, nor mount, nor dismantle, nothing was an obstacle for them.

They had seen extraordinary things, saved unbelievable difficulties, and felt fat, proud, and empowered to make the most bizarre decision that occurred to them.

In this state of emphasis, they saw a few hundred meters from them several cows detained on the side of the road, and heading there they reached the gate, closed with five robust sticks.

The cows were motionless, staring at the unreachable green paradise.

-Why do not they come in? The sorrel asked the cows.

-Because you cannot, they replied.

"We passed everywhere, " said the sorcerer haughtily . We've been everywhere for a month now.

With the brilliance of their adventure, the horses had sincerely lost the sense of time. The cows did not deign to even look at the intruders.

"Horses cannot, " said a quick heifer . They say that and do not go anywhere. We do go everywhere.

"They have rope, " an old mother added without turning her head.

- No, I do not have a rope! Responded the sorrel vividly . I lived in the capueras and passed.

-Yes, behind us! We passed and you cannot. The quick heifer intervened again:

-The boss said the other day: the horses with a single thread are

47

contained. And so...? Do not you guys pass?

"No, we did not pass, " the malacha replied simply, convinced by the evidence.

-Oh, yes!

To the honest malacara, however, it occurred to him suddenly that the cows, daring and astute, impertinent invaders of farms and the Rural Code, did not pass the gate either.

"This gate is bad, " objected the old mother. -He does! Run the clubs with the horns. -Who? Asked the sorrel.

All the cows, surprised by this ignorance, turned their heads to the sorrel. -The bull, Barigüí! He can more than the bad fences. - Wired ...? Pass? -All! Barbed wire too. We passed later.

The two horses, already returned to their peaceful condition of animals that a single thread contains, were naively dazzled by that hero capable of facing the barbed wire, the most terrible thing that can find the desire to move forward.

Suddenly the cows removed meekly: at a slow pace the bull arrived. And before that flat and stubborn front directed in quiet straight to the gate, the horses humbly understood their inferiority.

The cows moved away, and *Barigüí*, passing his head under a bar, tried to make her run to the side. The horses raised their ears, admired, but the bar did not run. One after the other, the bull proved his intelligent effort without success: the farmer, happy owner of the oat plantation, had secured the poles with wedges the previous afternoon.

The bull did not try anymore. Turning lazily, he sniffed in the distance, squinting, and then went along the fence, with drowned hissing hisses.

From the gate, horses and cows watched. In a certain place the bull passed the horns under the barbed wire stretching it violently upwards with his head, and the huge beast arched its back.

In four more steps he was among the oats, and the cows then went there, trying to pass. But the cows evidently lack the masculine decision to allow in the skin bloody scratches, and as soon as they introduced the neck, they quickly withdrew it with a dizzying nod.

The horses always watched.

"They do not happen , " he observed the malacha. They do not pass,

"The bull passed, " said the sorrel. Eat a lot. And the couple went in turn to pay for the fence by force of habit, when a clear and piercing bellow now, came to them: within the *avenal* the bull, with capers of false attack, bellowed before the farmer who with a Stick was trying to reach him.

-Ana...! I'm going to give you little jumps ... "the man shouted. Barigüí, always dancing and bellowing before the man, dodged the blows. They maneuvered fifty meters, until the farmer could force the beast against the fence. But this one, with the decision with the heavy and brute decision of its force, buried its head between the threads and passed, under a sharp *violineo* of wire and clamps thrown to twenty meters.

The horses watched as the man rushed back to his ranch, and came back out with a pale face. They also saw that the fence was leaping and was heading in their direction, so that the companions, before that determined step, moved back along the road in the direction of their farm.

As the horses marched docilely a few steps in front of the man, they were able to reach the bull owner's farm together, thus being able to hear conversation.

It is evident, from what follows from it, that man had suffered the unspeakable with the Pole's bull. Plantations, for inaccessible that they had been inside the mount; wired, however great their tension and infinite the number of threads, everything ran over the bull with its pillage habits. It also follows that the neighbors were fed up with the beast and its owner, by the incessant destruction of the former. But as the inhabitants of the region hardly denounce the Justice of the Peace, damage to animals, no matter how hard they are, the bull continued to eat everywhere except on his owner's farm, which, on the other hand, seemed to have a lot of fun with this. .

In this way, the horses saw and heard the irritated farmer and the *Polish cazurro*.

- It is the last time, Don Zaninski, that I come to see him for his bull! He just trampled all the oats. You cannot do it anymore!

The Pole, tall and with blue eyes, spoke with a sharp and sweet falsetto.

- Oh, bad bull! My cannot! My tie, escape! Cow is to blame! Toro is still cow!

- I do not have cows, you know well!

-No no! Vaca Ramírez! I'm crazy, bull!

- And the worst thing is that it loosens all the threads, you know it too!

-Yes, yes, wire! Ah, I do not know ...!

-Good! See, Don Zaninski; I do not want issues with neighbors, but have

For the last time be careful with your bull so that it does not enter through the bottom fence:

On the way I'm going to put new wire.

-Toro is on the way! No bottom!

-It is not going to happen by the way now.

- Come on, bull! Do not plectrum, not nothing! Everything happens!

-It will not happen.

-What does it say?

- Barbed wire ... But it will not happen.

- It does not do anything barb!

-Good; Do what you can because it does not enter, because if it happens it will hurt.

The chacarero left. It is like the previous evident that the malignant Pole, laughing once more of the animal's thanks, felt sorry, if possible as much as possible, for his neighbor who was going to build an insurmountable fence for his bull. Surely he rubbed his hands:

- Me they will not be able to say anything this time if bull eats all oats!

The horses resumed the road that led them away from their farm, and a little while later they arrived at the place where Barigüí had accomplished his feat. The beast was always there, motionless in the middle of the road, looking with solemn emptiness of ideas for a quarter of an hour, a fixed point in the distance. Behind him, the cows dozed in the hot sun, ruminating.

But when the poor horses passed by the road, they opened their eyes, contemptuous:

- It's the horses. They wanted to pass the fence. And they have rope.

-Barigüí yes happened!

- To the horses a single thread contains them.

-You are skinny.

This seemed to hurt the sorcerer alive, who turned his head:

-We are not weak. You are. It is not going to happen more here - it added pointing with the belfos the fallen wires, work of Barigüí.

-Barigüí always happens! After we passed. You do not pass.

-It's not going to happen anymore. The man said it.

-He ate the man's oatmeal. We passed later.

The horse, for greater intimacy of treatment, is appreciably more affectionate to the man than the cow. Hence, the malacara and the sorrel had faith in the fence that the man was going to build.

The couple continued on their way, and moments later, before the open field that opened before them, the two horses lowered their heads to eat, forgetting the cows.

Later, when the sun had just entered, the two horses remembered the corn and started back. They saw on the road the farmer who changed all the posts of his fence, and a blond man who, standing beside him on horseback, watched him work.

-I tell him what's going to happen -said the passenger.

"It will not happen twice, " replied the farmer.

-You'll see! This is a game for the damn Polish bull! It will happen! "It will not happen twice," the other repeated stubbornly. The horses continued, still hearing cut words:

-...laugh!

-...we will see.

Two minutes later, the blond man passed by with an English trot. The malacara and the sorrel, somewhat surprised by this step they did not know, watched the hurried man lose himself in the valley.

-Curious! -He observed the malacara after a long time -. The horse is trotting, and the man is galloping ...

They continued. At that moment they occupied the top of the hill, like that morning. Above the cold twilight sky, their silhouettes stood out in black, in gentle and downcast heads, the malacara in front, the sorrel behind.

The atmosphere, obfuscated during the day by the excessive light of the sun, acquired in that semi-shade an almost funereal transparency. The wind had stopped completely, and with the calm of the evening, when the thermometer began to fall rapidly, the frozen valley expanded its penetrating humidity, which condensed into a trailing mist in the dark depths of the springs. He relived, in the already cooled earth, the winter smell of burnt grass; and when the road paid for the mountain, the atmosphere, which felt suddenly colder and more humid, became excessively heavy with the scent of orange blossom.

The horses entered through the gate of their farm, for the boy, who was sounding the little box of corn, had heard his anxious trembling. The old sorrel got the honor of being credited with the initiative of the adventure, seeing himself gratified with a rope, for the purpose of what might happen.

But the next morning, quite late already because of the dense fog, the horses repeated their escape, crossing again the wild tabacal treading with mute steps the frozen pasture, saving the gate still open.

The sunlit morning, very high already, reverberated with light, and the excessive heat promised very soon a change of time. After crossing the hill, the horses suddenly saw the cows stopped on the road, and the memory of the previous afternoon excited their ears and their step: they wanted to see what the new fence was like.

But his disappointment, on arrival, was great. On the new posts - dark and crooked – there were two simple barbed wires, thick perhaps, but only two.

Despite his petty audacity, the constant life in the mountain farms had given the horses some experience in fencing. They watched carefully, especially the posts.

"They're made of wood, " said the malacha.

"Yes, burned pigs," the sorrel screened.

And after another long examination, the malacara added:

-The thread passes through the middle, there are no clamps ...

And the sorrel:

-They are very close to each other ...

Close, the posts, yes, undoubtedly: three meters. But instead, those two modest wires in replacement of the five threads of the previous enclosure, disillusioned the horses. How was it possible for the man to believe that the calf fence would contain the terrible bull?

"The man said it was not going to happen. " Malacara dared, however, that because he was his master's favorite, he ate more corn, for which he felt more believer.

But the cows had heard them.

- It's the horses. They both have a rope. They do not pass. Barigüí happened already.

-He passed? Here? Asked the malacha, disheartened.

-By the background. It happens here too. He ate the oatmeal.

Meanwhile, the loquacious heifer had tried to pass the horns between the threads; and a sharp vibration, followed by a sharp blow to the horns, left the horses in suspense.

"The wires are very stretched, " said the sorrel after a long examination.

-Yes. More stretched you can not ...

And both, without taking their eyes off the threads, thought dimly of how it could pass between the two threads.

The cows, meanwhile, encouraged each other.

-He happened yesterday. Pass the barbed wire. Us later

- Yesterday they did not happen. The cows say yes, and they do not pass, "the sorrel screamed. - There's a spike here, and Barigüí happens! There he comes!

Costing inside the mountain at the bottom, two hundred meters away, the bull was advancing towards the avenal. The cows were all facing the fence, keeping an eye on the invading beast. The horses, motionless, raised their ears.

- Eat all the oats! Then it happens!

-The threads are very stretched ... -he still observed the malacara, always trying to specify what would happen if ...

- He ate the oatmeal! The man comes! The man is coming! The loquacious heifer spoke.

In effect, the man had just left the ranch and was moving towards the bull. He had the stick in his hand, but he did not seem angry; He was very serious and with a contracted frown.

The animal waited for the man to arrive in front of him, and then he started the usual bellows, with feints of horns. The man advanced more, the bull began to retreat, always bellowing and sweeping the oats with his best capers. Until, ten meters from the road, he came back with a mocking mocking defiance challenge, and launched himself on the fence.

- Come Barigüí! Everything happens! It passes barbed wire! -The cows clamped.

With the impulse of his heavy trot, the huge bull lowered his head and buried his head between the two threads. There was a sharp moan of wire, a shrill screech spread from pole to pole to the bottom, and the bull passed.

But from his back and belly, deeply channeled from his chest to his rump, it rained rivers of blood. The beast, in stupor, was astonished and trembling for a moment. He walked away at once, flooding the grass with blood, until at twenty meters he lay down, with a hoarse sigh.

At noon the Pole went to look for his bull, and wept in falsetto before the impassive chacarero. The animal had risen, and could walk. But his owner, realizing that it would cost him a lot to cure him - if this was still possible -, he got him that afternoon. And the next day he was lucky to bring home two kilos of dead bull meat to his house in his suitcase.

THE MENSU

Cayetano Maidana and Esteban Podeley, pawns of obraje, returned to Posadas in the Silex with fifteen companions. Podeley, wood worker, returned at nine months, the contract concluded, and with free passage for free, therefore. Cayé - a month- old man - arrived in the same conditions, more than a year and a half, the time he had needed to cancel his account.

Skinny, disheveled, in his underpants, his shirt open in long slits, barefoot as most, dirty as all of them, the two mensú devoured with their eyes the capital of the forest, Jerusalem and Golgotha of their lives. Nine months up there! Year and a half! But they returned at last, and the ax that was still suffering from the life of the obraje was just a touch of splinters before the resounding pleasure that they sniffed there.

Of one hundred pawns, only two arrive at Posadas with haber. For that glory of a week that the river drags downstream, have the advance of a new contract. As an intermediary and coadjutant, he waits on the beach for a group of cheerful girls of character and profession, before whom the thirsty men threw their ahijú! of urgent madness.

Cayé and Podeley staggered down from a prearranged orgy, and surrounded by three or four friends found themselves in a moment before enough cane to fill the hunger for that of a mensu.

A moment later they were drunk, and with a new contract signed. In what work? Where?

They did not know, nor did they care. They knew, yes, that they had forty pesos in their pockets, and the faculty to reach much more in expenses.

Both drunks of rest and alcoholic bliss, docile and clumsy, both followed the girls to get dressed.

The warded maidens drove them to a store with which they had special relations of a few percent, or perhaps to the warehouse of the same contractor house. But in one or the other the girls renewed the detonating luxury of their rags, they nested the head of combs, they strangled themselves with ribbons - the whole thing with perfect cold blood to the gentleman alcohol of his mate, because the only thing that a mensú really possesses is a brutal detachment of your money.

For his part, Cayé acquired many more extracts and lotions and oils than necessary to burn his new clothes to nausea, while Podeley, more judicious, opted for a suit of cloth. Possibly they paid dearly for an account that was overheard and paid for with a pile of papers thrown on the counter. But anyway, an hour later, a brand new car was thrown at his new people, boots, a poncho on his shoulder - and a revolver in his belt, of course. -, replete the clothes of cigarettes that undo clumsily between the teeth, and dropping from each pocket the tip of a colored handkerchief. Accompanied by two girls, proud of that opulence, whose magnitude was accused in the somewhat weary expression of the mensú, dragging their car morning and afternoon through the hot streets, an infection of tobacco and extracts of obraje.

The night came at last, and with it the bailanta, where the same warned damsels induced the mensú to drink, whose royalty in money made them throw ten pesos for a bottle of beer, to receive instead a peso and forty cents, which they kept without even looking.

Thus, after constant waste of new advances - irresistible need to compensate with seven days of great lord the miseries of the obraje -, the mensú returned to rea up the river in the Sílex .

Cayé led a companion, and the three of them, drunk as the other laborers, settled next to the winery, where ten mules were crowded in close contact with trunks, tied, dogs, women and men.

The next day, with their heads cleared, Podeley and Cayé examined their notebooks: it was the first time they had done it since their contract. Cayé had received one hundred and twenty pesos in effect, and thirty-five in expenditure; and Podeley, one hundred thirty and seventy-five, respectively.

Both looked at each other with an expression that could have been frightening, if a mensu was not perfectly cured of it. They did not remember spending even a fifth part.

-Ana...! Cayé murmured . I will never fulfill ...

And from that moment he simply acquired - as a just punishment for his waste - the idea of escaping from there.

The legitimacy of his life in Posadas was, however, so evident to him that he was jealous of the major advance agreed upon with Podeley.

"You're lucky ... " he said . Great, your advance ...

"You bring a companion, " Podeley objected . That costs you for your pocket ...

Cayé looked at his wife; and although beauty and other qualities of a more moral nature weigh very little in the election of a mensu, he was satisfied. The girl dazzled, indeed, in her satin suit, green skirt and yellow blouse; He wore a triple pearl necklace on his dirty neck: he wore Louis XV shoes, his cheeks were brutally painted, and a disdainful leaf cigar under his half-closed eyelids.

Cayé considered the girl and her revolver 44: both were really the only things that were worth everything she had with him. And even the 44 was at risk of being shipwrecked after the advance, no matter how small was his temptation to carve.

On top of a trunk, in effect, the mensú played conscientiously to the mount whatever they had. Cayé observed a while laughing, as the peons always laugh when they are together, whatever the reason; and approached the trunk, placing a letter five cigars.

Modesto principle, which could provide enough money to pay the advance in the obraje and become in the same steam to Posadas, to waste a new advance.

Lost. He lost the other cigars, lost five pesos, the poncho, his wife's necklace, his own boots, and his 44. The next day he regained his boots, but nothing else, while the girl compensated the nudity of his neck with incessant scornful cigarettes .

Podeley won, after infinite change of owner, the necklace in question, and a box of scented soaps that he found a way to play against a machete and half a dozen stockings, which he won, thus being satisfied.

Finally, fifteen days later, they arrived at their destination. The pawns clambered up the endless red ribbon that climbed the ravine, from whose top the Chert It appeared tiny and sunk in the gloomy river. And with ahijús and terrible invectives in Guaraní, the mensú dismissed to the steam that had to drown, in a bucket of three hours, the nauseous atmosphere of desaseo, patchouli and sick mules, that during four days it overcame with him. For Podeley, a wooden laborer, whose diary could rise to seven pesos, the life of obraje was not very hard. Done to her, she tamed her aspiration of strict justice in the cubicaje of the wood, compensating the routine robberies with certain privileges of good pawn. His new stage began the next day, once his forest area was demarcated. He built with palm leaves his shed- roof and south wall, nothing else -; He gave the name of a bed to eight horizontal rods, and from a fork hung the weekly supply. He recommenced, automatically, his days of obraje: silent mates when getting up, at night still, that followed each other without giving off the hand of the turkey; the exploration in discovered wood; breakfast at eight o'clock, -harina (sour), charque and grease ; the ax then, to bare bust, whose sweat dragged gadflies, mosquitos and gnats; then lunch- this time beans and corn floating in the inevitable grease -to conclude at night, after a new struggle with the pieces of eight by thirty, with the yopara of noon.

Out of some incident with his farming colleagues, who invaded his jurisdiction; of the boredom of the days of rain that relegate him in crouches in front of the kettle, the task continued until Saturday afternoon. He washed his clothes then, and on Sunday he went to the store to provide himself.

This was the real moment of solace of the mensú, forgetting everything among the anathemas of the native language, coping with the indigenous fatalism the ever increasing rise of the provision, which then amounted to eighty cents per kilo of biscuit, and seven pesos for a boxer of canvas. The same fatalism that accepted this with a year! and a laughing look at the other companions, dictated, in elementary relief, the duty to flee from the work as soon as possible. And if this ambition was not in all the breasts, all the peons understood that bite of counter- justice that would, in case of arriving, to nail the teeth in the very heart of the pattern. This, on the other hand, took the fight to its final extreme, watching day and night its people, and especially the *mensualeros*.

Then the mensú would take place on the ironed, knocking pieces out between endless screaming, which rose from point to point when the mules, helpless to contain the prize that came down from the highest ravine at full speed, rolled over one another, tumbling, beams, animals, carts, all well mixed. The mules were rarely hurt; but the hubbub was the same.

I fell, between laughter and laughter, always meditated his flight. Already full of revirados and yoparas, that the prelude of the flight became more indigestible, still stopped by lack of revolver and, certainly, before the winchester of the foreman.

But if I had a 44! ...

Fortune came to him this time in a rather deviant way.

The companion of Cayé, that already deprived of his luxurious attire, earned a living washing the clothes of the laborers, changed a day of domicile. Cane waited for her for two nights; and the third went to the ranch of his replacement, where he gave a superb beating to the girl. The two mensú were alone chatting, friendly, as a result of which they agreed to live together, in which effect the seducer settled with the couple. This was economical and quite judicious. But as the mensú seemed to really like the lady -something rare in the guild -, Cayé offered it for sale by a revolver with bullets, that he himself would remove from the warehouse. Despite this simplicity, the deal was about to break, because at the last minute Cayé asked that a meter of tobacco be added to the rope, which seemed excessive to the mensú. The market finally came to an end, and while the newly married couple settled down on their ranch, Cayé was conscientiously carrying out his 44 to go to the end of the rainy afternoon, drinking mate with them.

The autumn ended, and the sky, fixed in drought with showers of five minutes, decomposed at last into constant bad weather, whose humidity swelled the shoulder of the mensú. Podeley, free of this until then, felt one day with such reluctance to reach his beam, which stopped, looking everywhere without knowing what to do. I had no heart at all. He returned to his shed, and on the way he felt a slight tingling in his back.

Podeley knew very well what that reluctance and the tingling of the skin meant. He sat down philosophically to drink mate and half an hour later a deep and long chill ran down his back.

There was nothing to do. The mensú threw itself on the rods shivering of cold, folded in trigger under the poncho, while the teeth, irrepressible, chattered to no more.

The next day the access, not awaited until the twilight, returned at noon, and Podeley went to the police station to ask for quinine. So clearly the pooch was denounced in the aspect of the mensú, that the clerk, without looking almost at the patient, lowered the packets of quinine.

Podeley calmly flipped over that terrible bitterness on his tongue, and when he returned to the mountain he stumbled upon the butler.

-You too! The butler said, looking at him . And there are four. The others do not matter ...

little thing. You are a compliant ... How is your account?

-It's not enough ... But I will not be able to hack ...

-Bah! Heal well and it's nothing ... See you tomorrow.

"Until tomorrow, " Podeley walked away, hurrying his way, because he had just felt a slight tingling in his heels.

The third attack began an hour later, leaving Podeley collapsed in a deep lack of strength, and his gaze fixed and opaque, as if he could not reach beyond one or two meters.

The absolute rest to which he gave himself for three days- specific balm for the mensu, for the unexpected -did nothing but turn him into a chattering, huddled bundle on a raggon. Podeley, whose previous fever had had an honest and regular rhythm, did not presage anything good for him from that gallop of accesses, almost without intermittence. There is fever and fever. If the quinine had not cut the second attack flush, it was useless to stay up there, to die in a ball at any bend in the chop. And went down again to the warehouse.

-Again you! -The butler received it. That's not right ... Did not you take quinine?

-I took ... I'm not with this fever ... I cannot with my ax. If you want give me for my passage, I'll fulfill as soon as I heal ...

The majordomo contemplated that ruin, and did not consider the life that It was in his pawn.

- How is your account? He asked again.

-I owe twenty pesos still ... On Saturday I delivered ...

I am very sick ...

-You know well that while your account is not paid, you must stay. Down... you can die Cure yourself here, and fix your account right away.

Heal a pernicious fever, where it was acquired? No, by the way; but the mensu that goes away may not return, and the steward preferred dead man to distant debtor.

Podeley had never failed to fulfill anything, the only arrogance that allowed a pattern of size before his employer.

-I do not care if you left or did not comply! Retorted the butler . Pay your bill first, and then we'll talk!

This injustice to him created, logically and quickly, the desire for revenge. He went to settle with Cayé, whose spirit he knew well, and both decided to escape next Sunday.

- There you are! The butler shouted to Podeley that same afternoon as he crossed paths with him . Last night three escaped ... That's what you like, is not it? Those were also compliers! Like you! But first you're going to burst here, get out of the iron! And be very careful, you and all who are listening! They already know!

The decision to flee and its dangers - for which the mensú needs all its forces - is capable of containing more than a pernicious fever. On Sunday, for the rest, it had arrived; and with false maneuvers of washing clothes, simulated guitars in this or that ranch, the surveillance could be mocked, and Podeley and Cayé suddenly found themselves a thousand meters from the police station.

As long as they did not feel persecuted, they would not abandon the bite,

Podeley walked badly. And even so... The peculiar resonance of the forest brings them, distant, a hoarse voice:

-To the head! To both!

And a moment later, the foreman and three pawns came running out of an elbow. The hunting began. Cayé cocked his revolver while continuing to flee.

-Get yourself, añá! Shouted the foreman from behind.

"Let's go in the woods," said Podeley . I do not have strength for me machete...

-I returned or shot you! Came another voice.

-When they are closer ... -repeated Cayé. A winchester bullet whistled through the bite.

-Enters! Shouted Cayé to his partner. And stopping behind a tree, he unloaded five shots of his revolver at the pursuers.

A sharp shout answered them, while another winchester bullet blew the bark of the tree that hid Cayé.

-Give yourself or I'll leave your head ...!

-And no more! He said. I fell to Podeley . I will... And after a new discharge, he entered the mountain. The persecutors, arrested for a moment by the explosions, raged forward, shooting, blow after blow of Winchester, the probable course of the fugitives.

A hundred meters from the bite, and following the same line, Cayé and Podeley moved away, bent to the ground to avoid the vines. The persecutors presumed this maneuver; but as within the mountain the attacker has a hundred odds against one being stopped by a bullet in the middle of his forehead, the foreman was content with winchester salvos and defiant howls. For the rest, the missed shots today had made nice white Thursday night ...

The danger had passed. The fugitives sat down, exhausted. Podeley wrapped himself in the poncho, and leaning on the back of his partner, suffered in two terrible hours of pooch, the backlash of that effort.

Then they continued the escape, always at the sight of the bite, and when the night arrived, they finally camped. Cayé had carried chipas, and Podeley lit fire, despite the thousand inconveniences in a country where, apart from the peacocks, there are other beings who have a weakness for light, without counting men.

The sun was very high already when the next morning they found the creek, the first and last hope of the escaped. Cayé cut twelve tacuaras with no neat choice, and Podeley, whose last forces were devoted to cutting the isypos, had barely time to do so before rolling over to shiver.

I fell, then, he built only the jangada- ten tacuaras tied longitudinally with lianas, carrying at each end one traversed.

Ten seconds later, they embarked. And the jangadilla, dragged adrift, entered the Parana.

The nights are excessively fresh at that time; and the two mensú, with their feet in the water, spent the night frozen, one next to the other. The current of the Paraná, that arrived loaded of immense rains, twisted the jangada in the borbollón of its eddies, and loosen slowly the knots of isipó.

The next day they ate two chipas, the last remaining provision, which Podeley barely tasted.

The tacuaras drilled by the tambums sank. And by late afternoon, the jangada had descended to a quarter of the water level.

Over the wild river, encased in the gloomy walls of forest, desert of the most remote woe, the two men, submerged to the knee, drifted spinning themselves, detained a moment motionless before a whirlpool, following again, just holding about the almost loose tacuaras that escaped from his feet, in a night of ink that could not break his desperate eyes.

The water reached their chest when they touched land. Where? They did not know ... A pajonal. But on the same shore they were motionless, stretched out on their bellies.

The sun was already dazzling when they awoke. The pajonal stretched twenty meters inland, serving as a coastline to river and forest. Half a block south, the Paranaí stream, which they decided to wade through when they had recovered their strength. But these did not return as quickly as it was to be desired, since the buds and worms of tacuara are fortifying tardies. And for twenty hours the rain closed transformed the Paraná into white oil, and the Paranaí into furious avenue. Everything impossible Podeley sat up suddenly dripping water, and leaning on the revolver to get up, pointed to Cayé. I was flying a fever.

-Pasá, añá! ...

Cayé saw that little could be expected from this delirium, and he leaned forward to reach his companion with a stick. But the other insisted:

- Go to the water! You brought me! Bandeá the river!

The livid fingers trembled on the trigger.

Cayé obeyed; He let himself be carried away by the current and disappeared behind the pajonal, which he was able to tackle with terrible effort.

From there, and from behind, he stalked his companion; but Podeley lay on his side again, knees drawn up to his chest, in the incessant rain. When approaching Cayé raised the head, and without abrir the patient the eyes, blinded by the water, murmured:

-Cayé, wow ... Very big cold ...

It rained all night on the dying man, the white and deaf rain of the autumn floods, until at dawn Podeley remained immobile forever in his water tomb.

And in the same pajonal, besieged seven days by the forest, the river and the rain, the survivor exhausted the possible roots and worms, lost his strength little by little, until being seated, dying of cold and hunger, with the fixed eyes in the Paraná.

The Flint , which passed by at dusk, picked up the already dying mensu. But his happiness transformed into terror when he realized, the next day, that steam was going up the river.

- Please, I ask you! He whined before the captain . Do not get off at Port X!

They're going to kill me! ... I'm really asking you! ...

The Flint returned to Posadas, taking him to the mensú, still drenched in nocturnal nightmares.

But within ten minutes of going ashore, he was already drunk with a new contract, and was staggering to buy extracts.

THE BEHEADED HEN

All day, sitting in the courtyard on a bench, were the four idiot children of the Mazzini couple- Ferraz. They had their tongues between their lips, stupid eyes and turned their heads with their mouths open.

The patio was of earth, closed to the west by a fence of bricks. The bench was parallel to it, five meters away, and there they remained motionless, their eyes fixed on the bricks. As the sun was hiding behind the fence, as the idiots declined they had a party. The blinding light caught his attention at first, little by little his eyes brightened; they laughed at last, loudly, congested by the same anxious hilarity, looking at the sun with beastly joy, as if it were food.

Other times, lined up on the bench, they hummed for hours, imitating the electric tram. The loud noises also shook their inertia, and they ran then, biting their tongues and mooing, around the patio. But almost always they were extinguished in a somber lethargy of idiocy, and they spent all day sitting on their bench, with their legs dangling and still, soaking their pants with glutinous saliva.

The oldest was twelve and the youngest eight. In all its dirty and helpless aspect was noted the absolute lack of a little maternal care.

Those four idiots, however, had once been the charm of their parents. After three months of marriage, Mazzini and Berta oriented their close love of husband and wife, and wife and husband, towards a much more vital future: a son:

What greater happiness for two lovers than that honest consecration of their affection, already freed from the vile selfishness of a mutual love without end none and, what is worse for love itself, without possible hopes of renewal?

This was how Mazzini and Berta felt it, and when the son arrived, after fourteen months of marriage, they believed their happiness was fulfilled. The creature grew, beautiful and radiant, until it was a year and a half old. But in the twentieth month, terrible convulsions shook him one night, and the next morning he did not know his parents anymore. The doctor examined him with that professional attention that is visibly looking for the cause of evil in the diseases of the parents.

After a few days the paralyzed members regained movement; but the intelligence, the soul, even the instinct, were gone altogether; He had been deeply stupid, slobbering, hanging, dead forever on his mother's knees.

- Son, my dear son! -She sobbed, on that awful ruin of her firstborn.

The father, desolate, accompanied the doctor outside.

-You can tell him; I think it's a lost case. You can improve, educate yourself in everything that your idiocy allows, but no further.

"Yes! ... yes! ... " Mazzini agreed. - But tell me: Do you think it's an inheritance, that ...?

- As for the paternal inheritance, I already told him what I believed when I saw his son.

Regarding the mother, there is a lung there that does not blow well. I do not see anything else, but there is a bit of a rough blow. Have her examine well.

With his soul shattered with remorse, Mazzini redoubled his love for his son, the little idiot who paid for his grandfather's excesses. He also had to console, relentlessly support Berta, hurt in the depths by that failure of her young motherhood.

Naturally, the marriage put all their love in the hope of another child. He was born, and his health and limpidity of laughter reignited the extinct future. But at eighteen months the convulsions of the firstborn were repeated, and the next day dawned idiot.

This time the parents fell into deep despair. Then his blood, his love were cursed! His love, above all! Twenty-eight years, he, twenty-two, and all his passionate tenderness did not manage to create a normal life atom. They no longer asked for more beauty and intelligence than in the firstborn; But a son, a son like everyone!

New flames of sore love sprang forth from the new disaster, a mad longing to redeem the sanctity of their tenderness once and for all. Twins ensued, and point by point the process of the two older ones was repeated.

But, beyond its immense bitterness, Mazzini and Berta had great compassion for their four children.

It was necessary to pluck the limbo of the deepest animality, not already their souls, but the instinct itself abolished. They knew swallowing, change places, or even sit. They finally learned to walk, but they ran into everything, because they did not realize the obstacles. When they washed, they moaned until their faces were injected with blood. They were encouraged only by eating, or when they saw bright colors or heard thunder. They laughed then, throwing out tongue and rivers of slime, radiant with bestial frenzy. They had, on the other hand, a certain imitative faculty; but nothing else could be obtained.

With the twins seemed to have concluded the terrifying descent. But after three years they wished another son ardently, trusting that the long time that had elapsed would have placated the fatality.

They did not satisfy their hopes. And in that fiery yearning that was exasperated, because of their fruitlessness, they soured. Until that moment each one had taken on himself the part that corresponded to him in the misery of his children; but the hopelessness of redemption before the four beasts that had been born of them, cast out that imperious need to blame others, which is the specific patrimony of the lower hearts.

They started with the change of pronouns: your children. And as the insult was more insidious, the atmosphere was charged.

"It seems to me," Mazzini said one night, who had just come in and washed his hands, "that you could have the boys cleaner."

Berta continued reading as if she had not heard.

"It's the first time, " he said after a while, "that I see you disturbed by the state of your children.

Mazzini turned his face a little to her with a forced smile:

-Our children, do I think?

-Good; of our children. You like it like that? -She raised

This time Mazzini expressed himself clearly:

-I think you're not going to say that it's my fault, right?

-Oh no! Berta smiled, very pale - but neither did I, I suppose! ... No more missing! ... – he murmured.

-What, did not lack more?

- That if someone is to blame, it's not me, understand it well! This is what I wanted to tell you.

Her husband looked at her a moment, with a brutal desire for a moment to insult her.

- Let's leave! He said, drying his hands at last.
-As you like; but if you want to say ...
-Bertha!
-As you like!

This was the first crash and was succeeded by others. But in the inevitable reconciliations, their souls were joined by double frenzy and madness by another son.

A girl was born that way. They lived two years with anguish to the flower of the soul, always waiting for another disaster. Nothing happened, however, and the parents put in her all their complacency, which the little girl took to the most extreme limits of mime and bad upbringing.

If even in recent times Berta always took care of their children, at birth Bertita forgot almost completely of the others. His only memory horrified her, like something atrocious that had been forced to commit. Mazzini, well, to a lesser degree, the same thing happened to him.

Not for that reason peace had reached their souls. The slightest indisposition of her daughter now cast out, with the terror of losing her, the grudges of her rotten offspring. They had accumulated gall over time so that the glass would not remain distended, and at the slightest contact the poison would pour out. From the first poisoned disgust they had lost respect; and if there is something to which man feels dragged with cruel fruition, it is, when it has already begun, to humiliate a person completely. Before they were contained by the mutual lack of success; now that he had arrived, each one, attributing it to himself, felt more the infamy of the four monsters that the other had forced him to create.

With these feelings, there was no longer any possible affection for the four older children.

The servant dressed them, fed them, put them to bed, with visible brutality. They hardly ever washed them. They spent most of the day sitting in front of the fence, abandoned from any remote caress.

In this way Bertita turned four years old, and that night, as a result of the treats that were absolutely impossible for the parents to deny, the baby had a chill and fever. And the fear of seeing her die or being an idiot, reopened the eternal wound.

They had not talked for three hours, and the reason was, as usual, the strong steps of Mazzini.

-My God! cannot you walk slower? How often?...
-Well, it's that I forget; it's over! I do not do it on purpose.
She smiled, disdainful:
-No, I do not believe you so much!
- Neither I, never, would have believed so much to you ... *tisiquilla*!
-What! what did you say?...

-Nothing!

-Yes, I heard you something! Look: I do not know what you said; but I swear I prefer anything to have a father like the one you've had!

Mazzini went pale.

-Finally! He muttered through clenched teeth. - Finally, viper, you said what you wanted!

-Yes, viper, yes! But I have had healthy parents! Do you hear ?, healthy! My father did not die of delirium! I would have had children like everyone else! Those are your sons, the four yours!

Mazzini exploded in turn.

-Thystic viper! That's what I told you, what I want to tell you! Ask, ask the doctor who is most responsible for the meningitis of your children: my father or your chopped lung, viper!

They continued with increasing violence, until a moan from Bertita instantly sealed their mouths. At one o'clock in the morning the slight indigestion it had disappeared, and as it happens fatally with all the young marriages that have loved each other intensely once, the reconciliation was restored, all the more effusive as the grievances were hurtful.

A splendid day dawned, and while Berta got up she spat blood. The emotions and last bad night had, without doubt, great guilt. Mazzini held her for a long time, and she cried desperately, but no one dared to say a word.

At ten they decided to leave after lunch. As they barely had time, they ordered the maid to kill a chicken.

The radiant day had ripped the idiots from their bank. So while the maid was slaughtering the animal in the kitchen, bleeding it out slowly (Berta had learned from her mother how to keep the meat fresh), she thought she felt something like breathing behind her. He turned around, and saw the four idiots, with their shoulders glued to each other, staring in amazement at the operation. Red

Red...

-Mrs! The children are here, in the kitchen.

Berta arrived; I did not want them to ever step there. And even in those hours of full forgiveness, forgetfulness and reconquered happiness, that horrible vision could be avoided!

Because, of course, the more intense the love abductions of her husband and daughter were, the more irritable was her more irritable mood with her humor with the monsters.

-Go out, Maria! Throw them! Throw them, I tell you! The four poor beasts, shaken, brutally pushed, went to give to their bank.

After lunch, they all left. The maid went to Buenos Aires, and the couple went for a walk in the fifth. When the sun went down they returned, but Berta wanted to greet her neighbors for a moment. His daughter escaped immediately home.

Meanwhile the idiots had not moved all day from their bank. The sun had already crossed the fence, began to sink, and they continued to look at the bricks, more inert than ever.

Suddenly, something interposed between his eyes and the fence. His sister, tired of five paternal hours, wanted to observe on her own. Stopped at the foot of the fence, looked thoughtfully at the crest. I wanted to climb, that did not doubt. At last he decided on a chair that had been demolished, but it was still missing. He then resorted to a box of kerosene, and his topographical instinct made him place the furniture vertically, with which he triumphed.

The four idiots, the indifferent look, saw how his sister patiently managed to dominate the balance, and how on tiptoe she rested her throat on the crest of the hill, between her straining hands.

They saw her look everywhere, and look for support with her foot to rise more. But the look of the idiots had been animated; the same insistent light

It was fixed in his pupils. They did not take their eyes off their sister, while the growing sensation of bestial gluttony changed every line of their faces. Slowly they advanced toward the fence. The little girl, having managed to put her foot on, was already riding astride and falling on the other side, surely, felt her leg catch. Beneath her, the eight eyes fixed on hers frightened her.

- Release me! let me! He shouted, shaking his leg. But she was attracted.

-Mom! Ow mom! Mom Dad! He cried imperiously. He still tried to hold on to the edge, but he felt torn and fell.

-Mom, oh! Ma ... "He could not scream anymore. One of them squeezed her neck, pulling back the loops as if they were feathers, and the others dragged her from one leg to the kitchen, where that morning she had bled to death to the hen, very subject, taking her life second by second.

Mazzini, in the house across the street, thought he heard his daughter's voice.

"I think he calls you, " he told Berta.

They listened, restless, but they did not hear anymore. However, a moment later they said goodbye, and while Berta was going to leave her hat, Mazzini advanced in the courtyard:

-Bitita!

Nobody answered.

-Bitita! The voice rose, already altered.

And the silence was so mournful for his always terrified heart that his back froze with horrible foreboding.

-My daughter, my daughter! He ran already desperate towards the bottom. But as he passed by the kitchen he saw a sea of blood on the floor. He pushed open the door ajar, and uttered a cry of horror.

Berta, who had already run away in turn at the anguished call of her father, heard the scream and responded with another. But as he rushed into the kitchen, Mazzini, as livid as death, stepped in, restraining her:

-D o not enter! Do not enter!

Be ta could see the blood flooded floor. He could only throw his arms over his head and sink along with a hoarse sigh.

Made in United States
North Haven, CT
13 June 2024